THE NINE DECISION

Kenny Figuly & Lenna Figuly

PublishAmerica
Baltimore

Hardcover 978-1-4560-6639-0
Softcover 978-1-4560-6640-6
PUBLISHED BY PUBLISHAMERICA, LLLP
www.publishamerica.com
Baltimore

Printed in the United States of America

DEDICATIONS

KENNY FIGULY: I dedicate this book to Kasey and Ryan for encouraging and believing in me when no one else would.

LENNA FIGULY: I dedicate this book to my children Leigh Ann and Andrew. Born January 5th 1983 and gone home to God June 15th 1986. You have my eternal love, Mom.

ACKNOWLEDGEMENTS

First and foremost we thank our unflagging editor Allan Shapiro. In the process of our writing this book he lent immeasurable time, effort and support without questioning the success of the project. Additionally, we thank Ryan Key and the rest of Yellowcard for the musical inspiration that drove our creativity and nearly destroyed our speakers as we wrote. Last, but certainly not least, our thanks and gratitude to Loretta Burdette and the rest of PA for presenting us with this opportunity.

THE
NINE
DECISION

CHAPTER 1 - THE XBRAIN

Cassie Lint bit the bottom end off her ice cream cone and let the cool chocolate liquid drizzle across her tongue. Standing at the edge of the school track, Cassie had timed her slow motion visual seduction perfectly. The boys of the varsity basketball team had just rounded the corner for their last lap, giving them a clear view of Cassie's head held back, her long blonde hair reflecting the sun's fire as it twisted and swung in the wind. Her eyes were closed, her tongue was seeking, and needless to say, it worked.

Matthew Brozik, who was at the head of the pack, momentarily lost his cadence, kicking one foot into the other as if his ankles had just been lassoed. Alfred Funkmaster, who was directly behind him, had no choice but to try and hurdle the falling Matthew, but since Alfred had been on a strict diet of Doritos and Ding Dongs ever since Coach told him he needed to bulk up, his leap carried him as far as Matthew's shoulders, or more accurately, onto Matthew's shoulders. Running directly behind Alfred was Steven Swanson, the team's center. He was too tall to do anything but put his arms out like Superman and fall face first. Finally, Donnie "Don't Call Me Dumbo"

Dumbowitz, who was still staring at Cassie with a smile on his face, snowballed into the other three.

Cassie tried to contain herself as the rest of the team ran in a 'V' formation around the wounded player pile, winking at her as they ran past. Frankie, however, was not amused.

"Great, sis," he said while shaking his head. "You just killed the basketball team."

"*What?*" Cassie said with laughter in her eyes. "Can't a girl have some fun?"

Frankie shot her a disapproving glance as she threw the remainder of the cone into a nearby garbage can. Being twins meant always having somebody who knew exactly what you were thinking, and though, for the most part, she couldn't be happier, there were times when Frankie used his mind-reading twin-superpowers to act as if he was her superior.

Cassie found it annoying but at the same time quite funny, especially since her brother thought the pinnacle of human achievement was the fart joke; and his best friend, Max, who happened to be the exact same age with the exact same birth date, still believed in Santa Claus despite seventeen years of obvious proof to the contrary. Max had a theory about Old Nick being stashed away in hanger 52 next to the aliens; Max was a conspiracy theorist at heart.

Cassie waved to the few stragglers still staring at her and enthusiastically waving back, causing Coach to blow his whistle. He yelled and stormed around the group telling them to keep their eyes focused on the task at hand and to ignore the pretty girls on the sidelines or he would ensure any number of cases of inflicted cranial rectal inversion. Cassie turned to her brother with a mischievous smile dimpling her cheeks and accentuating the ring of fudge around her mouth; like the latest in flavored lip liners.

"You know Frankie; it's not my fault that I'm irresistible."

"Yeah, sis," Frankie mumbled. "You have real goiter-appeal."

Cassie furrowed her brow and pursed her chocolate lips. "What's that supposed to mean?"

"Well," Frankie explained, trying to stifle his laughter, "you know how it is when you're on the bus and some real old woman gets on and she has this huge goiter hanging from her neck like a little baby's head? You know you shouldn't stare but you just can't help it because you keep waiting for that little goiter-baby to start talking or something?"

Cassie's brow furrowed so much her eyes were almost closed.

Frankie continued while holding in his laughter, "It's kind of like that."

"Shut up, dork!" she said while slapping his shoulder.

Frankie finally let out his laugh and turned around to scan the horizon. "Where is he already?"

As usual, Max was late. Every day, Frankie and Max had a three-hour window of time to get in some Xbox before their mother came home from work. Jeannie Lint was cool, by mom standards, but she hated video games. Frankie insisted she was missing out. She insisted that the world outside of the Xbox was where reality existed in all of its beauty and glory and that it was the ones on the Xbox that were missing out.

"What's more real than saving the world?" was his rebuttal. "The

Gears of War must turn. Marcus Fenix can't do it alone."

His rebuttal only seemed to prove his mother's point, causing a look on Jeannie Lint's face like someone trying to identify the source of a truly bad smell.

"I'm not waiting around, Frank," Cassie said with her arms crossed over her chest. "I need to get home and start my biology homework."

"Cassie, really! It's Friday! We have the whole weekend. And anyway, we can't just bail on Max because you've decided to be a major buzz kill." He shot her another glance; only this time it was far less playful than before. He was grumpy and hungry and he didn't own a car, so kissing up to Cassie for rides was a source of endless embarrassment and frustration for him.

"Hey, guys. Sorry I'm late," said Max as he rolled up on his skateboard. Max kicked back on the tail and the board shot up into his hands. "What?" he asked with suspicious caution.

"You're late, dill-hole!" Cassie accused as she started towards the parking lot situated next to the track.

"What's her problem?" Max asked Frankie, jerking his thumb in Cassie's direction. "And what's with that lipstick? It makes her look like a muppet."

Frankie responded to his friend with a snort and a nod. Then they dutifully followed Cassie to her car.

Cassie drove a fire engine red jeep with massive twenty-four inch tires, chromed-out roll-bar, and a lift kit that could intimidate the best of them. It took her three summers of yard work to save up for it. Three long, hot, heavy summers of sweat and dirt, of haggling with old people who had nothing better to do with their time than to check each blade of grass for uniform height, of listening to endless taunts from Frankie and Max as they would ride by on their bicycles telling her which spots she had missed, of doing nothing but working and eating and sleeping and saving. But it had all been worth it, and she would glow with a sense of pride whenever she would see her ride. This time, however, her glow was somewhat diminished by the fudge makeup she was wearing on her face.

As punishment for keeping her waiting, both Frankie and Max caught a small footed boot in the rear end as they made their way into the backseat, neither being allowed the privilege of riding shotgun.

"When's your mom getting home?" Max asked Frankie in a whisper, as they pulled out of the parking lot.

"We've got time, Maxie. I've moved it to the basement, just in case we're caught off guard."

Cassie shook her head with exaggerated contempt. Secretly she didn't give a crap what they did. They were boys, and in her years of taking mental notes, boys loved their toys. It started with water guns and GI Joes, and eventually graduated to fifty inches of television screen with plans for a plush in-home screening room not far behind.

"Boys will be toys," she giggled to herself as she drove with one hand on the steering wheel and the other holding onto the roll-bar. The intro to *Inferno* came through the speakers, which was inevitability turned up as loud as it could get, drowning out the muffled conversation from the backseat. *Odelay* was still her favorite album and she spent the rest of the drive home mouthing the words to each song and occasionally accompanying Beck in a duet when it was, in her opinion, critically necessary.

Soon the Lint home, a typical two story suburban Tudor for an atypical family, came into view. Frankie thought the reality of home was the world according to Xbox. Cassie thought the reality of home was its comfort whenever she woke from her secret recurring dreams that seemed too real to *be* dreams. Moments later Cassie's car screeched to a stop by the curb, causing an immediate ejection of the two boys from the backseat. Cassie followed lazily behind, turning to smile one last smile to her beautiful ride singing *Gold Chains* as she crossed the manicured lawn, *"I'm going back home with my gold chains swinging."* Then she was home.

The basement wasn't a bad deal. The air conditioning worked, the TV had cable and for all intents and purposes it was comfortable. It wasn't the Ritz, but it wasn't a dump either. Best of all it was off the beaten path hidden from other's prying ears.

Frankie set up the Xbox. He worked feverishly to complete the task at hand so they could get started. Cassie sprawled on the couch. It was a beta-gold and white thing their mom had found outside of an old furniture shop. Cassie relaxed with her head back against the armrest with her eyes half closed. Max sat next to Cassie, stealing glances of her.

"Go ahead and admit it. You're glad we're down here, hiding from your mom," Max stated as he picked up his controller and waved it at Cassie.

"I could not be more thrilled," Cassie said deadpan.

"I *am* the man!" Frankie struck a body builder stance after he rose from the floor after successfully re-cabling the Xbox. "It would be so much easier if everything was wireless, you know?"

Cassie narrowed her eyes at him as he pushed her legs out of the way and sat down between her and Max. "Yeah, that's just what we need; all of those wired signals floating around the ether. You think an Xbox knows the difference between a television and a brain?" Cassie said, elbowing her brother for forcing her to sit up.

"You'd need a brain first for there to be a difference," Frankie retorted, elbowing her back.

"Funny," she said flatly and removed herself from the now annoying company on the couch to the empty armchair beside it.

"That would be awesome," Max added.

"What?" Frankie asked, "If my sister had a brain?"

"No, if the Xbox could just be plugged *into* our brains."

"Like an Xbrain?"

"Exactly! Pretty brilliant, huh?"

Frankie nodded his head impressed. "No doubt! Hey, Cassie, call Japan and tell them to start working on the Xbrain. Oh, and then ask them to send over some shrimp tempura; I'm starving!"

Cassie shot him a full sized frown but she couldn't help chuckling too. "You guys are such dorks." But by then it was too late for them to have heard her. The war had begun again, and there was a whole wide world to save.

An hour later it was Frankie sprawling on the couch, trying to avoid thinking about how they were spending another Friday night. He couldn't help but wonder if he and Max had become introverts without realizing it.

No matter how hard he tried to put it out of his mind he realized the last few weekends were spent doing the exact same thing; playing some stupid game in a cold, weathered basement.

Max gave Frankie a knowing glance. "I bet you were up all night thinking about this very moment," he said as he moved to sit more comfortably on the floor. "You think it'll ever happen that a couple of hot chicks will walk by and notice that we're in your basement?"

Frankie looked puzzled in the same way a dog does; tilting his head as if hearing the sound of sirens in the distance. "*I think I hear them now,*" thought Frankie.

"Do *you* hear the sirens Max? " Frankie asked him. Max tilted his own head and looked up from the floor at Frankie and whined like a puppy. They both laughed.

Cassie clattered down the basement stairs carrying cookies. She walked over to the couch and sat down next to Frankie as she munched a couple of the Oreos. "You guys will never get laid playing video games," Cassie observed.

Both Max and Frank ignored her. They knew what they were about. They were well aware that at this moment in both their lives they were much better at war than women.

"Don't you guys ever get bored doing the same old thing?" asked Cassie. "I'm thinking we should do something different for a change. Maybe we should all go away; far, far away."

"Frankie Lint?" queried a voice from upstairs. "This is your mother speaking. If you and Max are down there playing video games before your homework is finished I'm taking that expletive box and throwing it away."

Both boys froze, assuming that stillness equaled invisibility.

Cassie took the Oreo that she was about to take a bite out of and tossed it into the air. When the cookie succumbed to gravity it landed hard, hitting Frankie in the back of the head. Frankie looked over at her with a scowl while maintaining his invisibility-silence.

"Hi, mom, it's me Cassie, your dutiful daughter. I have no idea where the boys are. As far as homework is concerned, mine is done."

"That's crap," said Jeannie. "Max? Go home. You can come back when your homework is done and when my son has learned the meaning of the word priorities."

Max looked at Frankie. He smiled. Frank didn't.

"I'll get right on that, Mrs. Lint." Max responded while trying to hold off his laughter. He finally glanced at his friends with a look in his eyes of a little boy sneaking off with his daddy's last cigarette.

Frank, Max and Cassie scurried their way up the stairs. Jeannie was at the top, arms folded and a smile on her face. "It's a good thing you two have me or you would both be failing by now." She gave her son a playful smack on the behind and led Max to the front door.

Jeannie could not imagine any circumstance in which Cassie or Frankie would allow themselves to fail at anything. But like any mother, a riot of bizarre thoughts often toppled through her head. These were the what-ifs in life. Ever since the recent death of her husband there was an uncomfortable amount of common ground between living and loss. Gobbling up pain as though it were something edible but not very pleasing to the palate, Jeannie was on guard for the safety of her children twenty four hours a day, seven days a week; chewing on grief and spitting out the bad bits as she became used to the circumstances of their newly diminished existence.

She knew that life had to be devoured as it presented itself to be truly appreciated, but when it came to her children she was a deliberate hypocrite. Therefore, homework and dinner were on the agenda before play and for late Friday afternoon, the gears of war ground to a halt.

CHAPTER 2 - THE PREGNANT VAMPIRE

The next morning, Cassie woke to a rogue stream of yellow light coming like a flood through a crack in the curtains. The clock was on her nightstand. She knew exactly where it was. She knew that all she had to do to know the time of day was to roll over onto her side. But she couldn't. She wouldn't. Knowing what time it was meant having to do something about what time it was. So, she lay on her back and stared. The sunlight formed a single line upon her ceiling, dividing it into two equal parts. One part for what was possible should she get up, the other for what could be impossibly accomplished asleep. Lucky for Cassie, she knew there was a third option: the line that separated the two, and that was where she decided to stay, at least until there was someplace else to go.

"So much to do," she thought. *"So much not to do,"* sighed Cassie. *"I can do anything,"* she thought. *"I can do nothing. I am the cameraman in the zombie movie because the one holding the camera never dies. I'll live forever, searching all over the world for the only boy left with a brain. I hope he's cute,"* she sighed. Cassie thought of one more criteria, *"and I really hope he's a cameraman too."*

Strange thoughts for Cassie, who normally was quite motivated to do something, even if it was just watching Frankie and Max, pretend to be grown men. However, something had been happening lately, some feeling carrying through her dreams and into her days. Now it was Saturday and the whole world awaited her out her front door, but all she wanted to do was stare at the sun. "*If only something different would happen*," she thought. "*If only I owned a really good camera*," she dreamt. "*If only the phone would stop ringing.*"

"Am I the only one alive in this house," Cassie groaned before finally getting out of bed to answer the phone.

"Do you have any idea what time it is?" she answered without saying hello.

It was Max. "Yeah," he answered. "It's 11:30."

"11:30? Are you sure?" Cassie responded to Max.

"Yeah, really," Max continued. "And I'm glad it's you, because get this..."

"Hey, Max," Cassie interrupted, still marveling at how late it was and wondering just how long she spent staring at a ray of light. "How come the cameraman never gets killed in zombie movies?"

"Because the electromagnetic waves from the camera disguises the cameraman's brainwaves from the zombies," Max answered without missing a beat before adding, "Duh."

"Huh," Cassie said impressed.

"Why? Has the outbreak started? Has it gotten Frankie yet? I'm asking because he might be the *only* person to become smarter *after* being zombified."

"No kidding," Cassie agreed with a chuckle. "What were you going to say?"

"When Cass?" Max asked, confused.

"Before I asked about the zombies," Cassie said impatiently. "You said you were glad I answered because…"

"Oh right!" Max interrupted excitedly. "You remember that trip last year that was all planned but then got cancelled?"

"You mean the trip to Israel?" she said, feeling her excitement rising.

"Right! I mean totally! Well, guess what?"

"No way!" squealed Cassie with delight.

Cassie could imagine Max nodding his head and grinning on the other end of the phone. "Right on! Now that things are cool over there again, it's back on! Can you believe it? Freaking Israel! It would be so awesome!"

Cassie could hardly contain her excitement. "Yeah, but my mother would *never* let Frankie and me to do anything as crazy as that. She has a hard enough time just letting us hang out at the mall after nine o'clock" Cassie paused. Positive and negative thoughts were colliding with each other in her head, giving off tiny explosions of happiness and disappointment like bubbles popping in her brain. Would her mom let her and Frankie go? Would she ever get a chance like this again? Would this be the one thing to make all the other things make sense? Would Frankie really eat her brains if he was the first one to be turned into a zombie? Would she eat his? Cassie's mind had wandered from her conversation with Max.

"Are you still there?" came Max to wake her from her daze.

Cassie shook her head of her thoughts. "Yeah…whatever… I was just thinking."

"Good luck with that," Max said sarcastically.

Cassie made a face at the phone, but before she had a chance to make an equally sarcastic reply such as "Shut up moron," Max asked to talk to Frankie.

"Yeah, sure, hold on," Cassie said, too excited to think of something clever to say, running out of her room and down the stairs. Through the sliding glass doors that led to the backyard she could see her brother sitting by the pool. He was skinny, maybe too skinny, and with his pale skin and light brown eyes, he practically blended into the white cushion of the lounge chair.

"Hey dork," said Cassie, sarcastically. "It's for you."

"Who is it?"

"That's easily the stupidest question you've asked all year." Cassie met her brother halfway, handing him the phone. "And when you're done, we've got to start planning!"

"Planning? For what?" Frankie asked as he took the telephone from his sister.

"You'll see!" Cassie was growing more excited by the second. "But here's a hint. What's the opposite of *it ain't real*?"

"*The opposite of it ain't real?*" Frankie scrunched up his face in confusion as he put the telephone to his ear. "What do you mean by it ain't real?" he asked Max. Then, finally, as Cassie was already making a full sprint back to her room, she heard Frankie yell out in triumph, "Israel!"

Much of the next week was spent in the planning stages. The boys agreed that it would be Cassie who talked to Jeannie. Max knew his parents would have no problem with him leaving for the summer; they were always busy anyway and Max had grown quite adept at playing the guilt card. Max's father, the state's Attorney General, believed life must be experienced to be fully appreciated.

It built character.

It built distance.

Distance from exactly what, Max was never quite sure, but it worked in his favor.

Cassie and Frank had no such luck, however. Every argument their mother could come up with had to have a foolproof counter-argument, and then a counter-counter argument for their mother's counter-argument that was sure to follow. Research needed to be collected; witnesses prepared; judges bribed. They even toyed with the idea of doing a Power Point presentation to present their case professionally and in a responsible way.

Finally, the big day arrived; that Thursday. Jeannie Lint was always in a particularly good mood after watching *The Office*, her favorite television show, and everything would have been perfect if Frankie hadn't freaked out and spent nearly a half an hour barraging his mother with nonsensical chatter. Cassie didn't want to seize him by the arm, spin him around and slap him silly, but she would if she had to. When Cassie Lint set her mind to something, nothing was going to stand in her way, not even her babbling brother.

"Hey Frankie," she finally said. "Why don't you go do something stupid and leave us alone for a minute?"

Frank, who was in the middle of explaining the pagan origins of the Easter Bunny, turned red-faced to Cassie to mouth the word "sorry" before quickly excusing himself. Being Frankie he made sure to flick his sister on the top of the head as he left the room.

Jeannie Lint, who was more than just a little privy to her children's behavior turned the television off to offer her full attention to her daughter. She knew something big was coming. Jeannie smiled a nervous smile, followed by a deep breath. It was only then when she turned to Cassie who stood stoically in the middle of the living room.

Cassie opened her mouth to begin her opening arguments, but her mother beat her to the punch.

"Are you pregnant?"

Cassie opened her eyes in shock.

"Lord, mother, you have to know me better than to even *consider* that possibility!"

Obvious relief spread over Jeannie's face, which was immediately followed by a sharp tinge of guilt for having thought the worst. She tried to lighten the mood.

"Are you a vampire?"

Cassie, still red with embarrassment, relaxed as well.

"No, mom, I'm not a vampire."

Jeannie nodded her head.

"Well... are you a pregnant vampire?"

"Vampires can't get pregnant, mom," Cassie answered wondering on what planet her mother had grown to adulthood.

Jeannie nodded her head again and said, "Oh, right." Then she patted the seat next to her indicating she wanted Cassie to sit down. "So what is it?" she asked as her daughter sat next to her.

"Mother, just listen please. Listen to everything I have to say before you say no. Before you hear my entire thoughts it would not be fair for you to make a judgment, or a decision, or whatever. You know what I mean." Cassie shifted nervously, crossing one leg over the other and then back again, inwardly cursing for forgetting everything they had planned for that week.

Cassie smiled in a big way and knew it was too big a smile to flash at her mom.

"I'm all ears, sweetheart." Her mother looked into Cassie's eyes; the expression on her face seemed to be a cross between the Cheshire cat and Judge Judy.

"There's a million ways I can say this, but I think I'm just going to spit it out." Cassie thought for a moment, staring up at the ceiling. She noticed a spitball that Frankie had shot there about ten years ago. Cassie composed herself. "A group of teachers have decided to join an archaeological dig in Israel. There are already several kids our age going and I'd love it, I mean I would really, really love it, if you would consider allowing me and Frank to go as well... to Israel... consider it, please mom... us going."

It was said. The deed was done. And though Cassie could obviously see her mother's eyes double in size, nothing as of yet came out of her mouth. "*So far so good,*" Cassie thought, "*unless the reason she isn't speaking is because I just gave her a stroke.*"

It took a few minutes, but Jeannie Lint did blink, which resulted in a wave of relief spreading over Cassie's face, mostly because she was actually starting to worry that she had given her mother a stroke.

Jeannie finally spoke. "You guys are going to be eighteen next year. You probably already know that what you're asking scares the hell out of me." Jeannie paused for a moment. She closed her eyes. She folded her arms and took a deep breath. So many things invaded her mind, so many things to worry about, so much that could go wrong if she said yes or if she said no. The one thing that stuck out among all the things swirling around in her mind was her husband, Cassie and Franks' father, and how if he were still alive, the answer would have been so easy. The fact that it wasn't only confirmed how much they all needed a change; her especially.

Jeannie took a deep breath, wiped the tears that had formed in her eyes and said simply, "You can go." And then, "Now get away from me so I can have a good cry."

Cassie stood up and looked at her mother crying. Cassie was crying too but she knew they were crying good tears. She also knew this was not the time to comfort her mother. This was a hard gift for her to give and the only way to receive it was to walk away. As Cassie left the room she grew more and more excited. They were going to Israel. They were going to the Holy Land. They were going to walk the same streets as Jesus. And, for whatever reason, she felt like she was taking the first step toward getting the answer to a question that she didn't have the courage to ask herself yet.

CHAPTER 3 - MEAT INCENSE

Cassie craned her body forward and leaned her head against the glass. This was only the second time she and her brother had flown anywhere, and takeoffs were always the hardest part. Watching as the land fell beneath them, rising further and further from the only world they've known, Cassie always considered flying a little bit like being born. It was noisy, scary, and for all those involved, life would never be the same again.

The first time she and Frankie went anywhere was a year ago, after their father's death. Their uncle was a paraplegic who lived in Pennsylvania. He couldn't make it to the funeral and since he had never met his niece and nephew he figured having them visit was as good a time as any. That first time traveling felt like being born too, like becoming somebody else. In that case she went from being her father's daughter to her uncle's niece; not a change she was very happy to make. Nor did she feel bad for her paraplegic uncle when she finally met him. In fact, if asked, she would say that she didn't like him at all. Cassie was never good at hiding how she felt. She was a bad actress and she knew it.

Soon, without noticing it, Cassie drifted off into the safe arms of sleep.

Was it a dream?

She wasn't sure.

There was something odd about the way things were happening; as if they were working backwards in the dark. Sure enough she was sitting on the plane. To her left were Frank and Max. The lights in the great beast were dim and most of the passengers were asleep.

Cassie unbuckled her seatbelt and stood up. There was something missing, something important to the scene that would've made it seem more real and not so disconnected.

She couldn't place it. The people were there. The casual bump and slide of the plane riding the jet stream played slightly on her balance but it was not a cause for alarm.

Cassie carefully moved past Frankie and Max and into the aisle. She decided it was time to visit the bathroom. Although it wasn't a pleasant thought, it was something to do.

As she made her way down the aisle she figured out what was wrong, what was missing from the picture. It was sound, or lack thereof. Panic filled her body. She tried to pop her ears. Perhaps the pressurization had affected her in a more profound way than everybody else, she thought. Perhaps she was just more sensitive to such things. Perhaps the recent inane chatter of Frankie and Max would be the last sounds she would ever hear. A frightening thought to say the least. But her ears did pop, and there was no pain, and there seemed to be nothing wrong with them at all.

Cassie took a deep, silent breath in the hope it would calm her.

She realized that everything has an explanation, so she strained as hard as she could to hear. The sleeping baby next to her in row 30D, the baby was breathing, wasn't it? After all, only dead babies refused to breathe. She could plainly see the baby's chest slowly rise and fall in the rhythm of life. *"Remember, Cassie,"* she told herself, *"only dead babies refuse to breathe."* She was starting to panic again.

Still, there was no sound.

Not a whisper.

Not. A. Sound.

Nothing.

In fact, even the engines failed to make the slightest noise.

"Think hard Cassie!"

"Are you dreaming?"

She made her way to the back of the plane, pausing here and there to make sure that the sleeping passengers were in fact alive. They all seemed to be oblivious to the world as she was experiencing it.

"Don't be stupid! Knock on something. Say something. Create your own sound, your own reality."

Cassie walked the length of the aisle and knocked on the bathroom door.

Knock, knock, knock!

There it was. It was there; a sound that rose clearly above the silence.

Cassie let out a heavy sigh, realizing the entire time she'd been holding her breath. It felt good to breathe. It felt good to fill her lungs full, but the rest of it still didn't make sense.

She opened the door to the restroom, entered, and locked it behind her. The reflection in the mirror caught her off guard. It was her, but somehow it reflected the feelings and emotions of someone else; some other girl.

She looked closer. It was the eyes. They were different. They were brown, dark brown, but different. Perhaps they were a bit too tired, or fearful? They were her eyes, but instead of being a nice chocolate brown, they were black and empty. And then, in a heavy, terrified realization, Cassie knew she was looking into the eyes of someone else altogether, someone who hated her and wanted her dead.

Reaching for the door, she unlocked it and ran out heading back towards her seat. The passengers were still asleep. There was still no noise. And then, in the corner of her eye, she saw him.

A man.

A dark man.

He was very tall and thin and dressed all in black; wearing a top hat and suit coat.

It wasn't the way he was dressed that was so disturbing, although she wasn't about to allow that bit to go unnoticed. It was his lanky, disproportionate arms and fingers. They were too long for his height and too thin for his weight. His bony wrists extended from the sleeves, followed by fingers that seemed to be made of branches from a dying tree. His skin was gray skin, dead skin, seen as white in a ray of light. It seemed as if this man wanted to, from no matter where he stood, could lift up his arm, reach out his hand, and take her very soul.

Before she could blink he was standing by her side. His breath was deep, musty and sickeningly sweet. Later she would describe it as "meat incense." Cassie's mind raced to find reason, but there was nothing. Between the smell of his rotting breath and the obvious disjointed reality of his existence, Cassie could barely hold on.

And then, finally, she awoke.

It was only a dream, but it wasn't only a dream. She knew it wasn't only a dream. Cassie Lint knew it was a warning.

She jumped as the sound of the landing gear clicked into place, tucking herself in as the jet engines thrust the massive machine forward. She tried not to think about what it would be like to hit the ground at five hundred and fifty miles an hour and burst into flames. It wasn't so much the idea of death that frightened Cassie; it was the dying part that she didn't like; especially if it came from falling thirty-eight thousand feet.

The sound of the engines flattened slightly as the plane equalized and Cassie decided she was okay. A moment ago she had been afraid of becoming a speeding, fleshy, one hundred and fifteen pound fireball and her alarm was now soothed by the shallow chattering of Max and Frankie.

She giggled quietly to herself, as the two boys reminded her of a couple of old women discussing cake recipes. She enjoyed their company. And even though she wasn't part of the "guy club"; not that she would want to be, she was comfortable in her position as the obvious brains of the family.

After a three hour layover at London Heathrow and nineteen overall hours of flight time, the three travelers were eager to get off the plane at Ben Gurion International Airport and find a place to gather their wits.

Max, Cassie, and Frank made their way through Customs at breakneck speed. Less than an hour after landing, they were finally free and open to new experiences.

Mrs. Ford, their sociology teacher, brought everybody together and made a headcount. Five kids, including the three of them, were present and accounted for.

"Okay, everyone, I need your attention." Mrs. Ford, in all her kindness, looked frazzled, but years of dealing with pubescent teens had taught her to keep her composure, no matter how much she wanted to cover her ears and scream. This instance was no different, and instead of meeting inattentiveness with anger, she closed her eyes, said a quick Serenity Prayer to herself and then took control of the situation.

"If I don't have everybody's attention right now this instant," she majestically announced, "I am turning this plane around and we're going home."

Silence descended on the group, as if time had stopped, and all eyes turned to the one who had stopped it.

It was Frankie who broke the silence. "Um, Mrs. Ford?"

"Yes, Frankie?" Mrs. Ford answered after taking a deep breath through her nose.

Frankie moved his eyes slowly around the airport, unsure whether to say what he was about to say. "Um...we're not on the plane anymore."

Mrs. Ford smiled and nodded her head. "Seems the devil is in the details," she said more to herself than to him. "But you see my point, yes?" which was directed at all of them.

They all nodded their heads and chorused, "Yes."

"Good! Now I need to collect your passports and the paperwork that you filled out at the beginning of the flight. Once we have everything in order we are going to board the van outside that has the yellow flag sticking up out of the back end. Got it?"

"Got it," came the chorus.

Mrs. Ford, along with a couple of the other kids, proceeded to load the luggage on the luggage carrier.

"Who wants to help push this?" she asked as she lifted the heaviest one onto the pushcart. Cassie admired her strength. She knew that if anyone ever asked her what kind of person she aspired to be like, she'd have no problem referring to Mrs. Ford.

Kyle and Ryan offered to help without hesitation. Kyle was something of a surfer boy with beach-blond hair and that easy view of life as if all one needed to be happy was a good wave. Ryan was a redhead, which seemed to define much of his personality. His cheeks wore a practically perpetual blush. Everything seemed to embarrass him, whether it was answering a question in class, walking down the hall, or talking to a girl. He started getting pink when standing next to a girl, or even thinking about a girl; excellent reasons why his skin had been bright red since the start of the trip. Cassie seemed to have that affect on boys, regardless of the color of their hair.

Everybody liked Kyle and Ryan, especially Cassie who thought they were hilarious. Max got along well with them too. For some reason, however, Frankie turned his nose up at them as often as possible. Cassie thought he was secretly jealous of them. But her brother, being the guy he was, would never admit to something like jealousy over another guy.

"Hey, Max," said Kyle. "Can you believe we're really here? Freaking Israel! Who would have thunk it?" Kyle patted Max on the back and then continued to load their cart.

"I've got to say, Kyle, this is really a mindblower!"

Max picked up his backpack and opened the top, pulling out his diabetes kit. He hadn't checked it in over a day. Usually, it was no big deal to go a day without checking as long as he remembered to give himself a shot of insulin every twenty-four hours. He checked. His level was fine, as he knew it would be.

"Hey, Max," said Frank, "what do you think would happen if we filled that needle full of insulin and stuck it in Kyle's ear? Think we could give his brain diabetes?" Frank said it loud enough that Kyle could hear him.

"Here you go, Frankie. I brought this for you." Kyle reached into the left-hand pocket of his jeans and whipped out his middle finger. Both boys laughed, knowingly. The tension was there, in secret, but so was the friendship. They liked it that way. They liked the game. And even though they knew that most were in on their little diversion, it was still fun to pretend.

Max failed to see the humor. He shot Frank a hard look and proceeded to put away his diabetes kit. Max hated being a diabetic. Frank knew he hated it. Of course, most of the time Max loved his best friend's humor; this time it wasn't funny.

Frankie felt awful. He casually ambled over to Max and gave him a big embrace. He knew that words were not enough at that moment so he kept his mouth shut. Frankie was sure he would only say the wrong thing and add insult to injury.

Emotions were running high. They were exhausted and worn out. By the time they loaded up the van and made it to the youth hostel on the edge of the town, the expired day lay buried beneath their pillows.

CHAPTER 4 - THE MAN MADE OF SHADOWS

Her disciplined mind almost rebelled as she stood at the edge of the world and looked down. She had hoped to find peace there, but dreams can sometimes be relentless and wicked, even when the message is sacred.

He was standing in the doorway, this man made of shadows and rotting meat. He was at least 7 feet tall and gave the impression of height and strength beyond anything she had ever recognized before; his dark, angry eyes seemed to convey a promise of an unnatural doom.

There were voices too. Hungry voices as if from hungry mouths, broken and breathless. Horrible sounds of hunger, yet somehow devouring not only each other, but the very air around them. This time, however, Cassie felt better, because she knew what was happening; she knew it was only a dream. And though the voices were horrible, were the worst thing she had ever heard, at least she could hear. At least this time, since she knew it was only a dream, she could treat it as such. She needed to understand why this was happening to her.

But as he entered the room that same stench of rotting flesh and patchouli washed over her, and her mind raced in fear. It's all just a dream, she told herself. But it didn't feel like a dream; it didn't feel like anything she'd ever experienced before.

She pretended she was asleep, thinking how strange it was to pretend to be asleep while actually being asleep, which only made her wonder if she was really asleep. She forced her eyes into slits. She told herself it wasn't real.

And she watched.

And she knew.

She knew she wasn't dreaming at all.

"Please, dear God, make this a dream."

The man was already in the room, slowly turning his head from one side to the other as if he was searching for something. There was no available light, and yet, somehow, this thing, this man, was darker than the darkness itself. He cast shadows upon shadows.

"How is this possible?" Cassie thought in wonderment.

He moved about the room and Cassie watched with one eye barely open. In the darkness she knew his very presence would snuff out even the brightest midday sun.

He made his way to the edge of her brother's bed and looked down. Her brother, caught somewhere in a dream, took a sudden deep breath and fell blindly back into the sweet arms of sleep. She loved Frank. Frank was all the color she had in a black-and-white world. She wanted to scream. She wanted to make this harbinger of death a lesser thing than terror.

Then, suddenly, he glanced at her. He knew she was watching. And somewhere beneath the black, Cassie sensed the man was smiling at her, that he was mocking her. She hated him. He lifted his right hand, and without moving his body his shadowy arm stretched across the room and touched her lips as gently as a mother would touch the lips of her newborn child.

The pain and the fear from his touch were excruciating. There was no air to scream; no experience she could use for comparison.

Just as suddenly as the shadowy man had appeared, he was gone.

"Holy crap," said Ryan from somewhere in the room.

Ryan's outburst caught her off guard

"It smells like a freaking fart city in here," he continued. "God, I hope that wasn't you Cassie." Ryan stood up and turned on the lights. The rest of the gang, completely absorbed in sleep, woke immediately with the same revolting look on their faces.

"I wonder if Mrs. Ford's room smells just as nasty," offered Kyle with a snicker.

"I wonder if it's just your upper lip, Kyle," said Max. All four boys began laughing hysterically. Cassie decided then and there that whatever was haunting her would have to remain a secret. How could she possibly explain such a thing?

"Hey, that's pretty funny coming from someone who's never funny," said Kyle.

"Does anybody know what time it is?" asked Cassie. She was tired but she was also inexplicably hungry.

"4:30 AM, local time," said her brother. Half-naked he walked across the room in his SpongeBob boxer shorts and looked through the window out into the early morning. There was nothing there,

36

except for a strange looking man across the street smoking a cigarette.

"I'm starved," said Cassie.

"Yeah, I could go for some Taco Bell just about now," said Ryan.

The thing about Ryan was that he was always hungry. The other thing about Ryan was that he always wanted Taco Bell.

Cassie got out of bed and offered to go find Mrs. Ford.

"No Taco Bell for Ryan. It's my guess he's the one that made the whole room smell like crap; worse than crap. Like real, actual crap," said Kyle.

"We get it, freak!" said Max.

Cassie pulled a hoodie over her t-shirt and walked out of the room. The hallway of the hostel was lit by several strands of blue and gold rope-light, which cast a dim glow along the ceiling. It seemed a lot longer now than when they first arrived, but perhaps she was just too tired to notice. There also seemed to be more doors than she remembered. Six rooms could be accessed through their closed doors. Only the bathrooms had doors that were open.

Cassie deliberately left the door to the room slightly ajar. Staring down the hall, longer than it was, with more closed doors than it needed, Cassie didn't know what to think anymore; the dream that was not a dream, the man that was not a man, and a touch that was so much more than a touch. How was she supposed to make sense of anything anymore?

Cassie wasn't sure which room Mrs. Ford was in. She figured it would be the one closest to theirs and she tapped on it three times. She could hear movement from within.

Mrs. Ford opened the door, squinting, and looking quite puzzled.

"Cassie," she began, "Are you okay?" She led Cassie into her room and shut the door behind her.

The room was much smaller than she would've imagined. She wondered why Mrs. Ford wasn't sharing a room with one of the other female professors. It didn't matter. The best part of Mrs. Ford's room was that it felt safe and inviting. It smelled nice. If she were a girly girl, Cassie would have asked to stay.

"Mrs. Ford, the five of us are pretty hungry."

"You know it's funny you should say that, I was getting pretty hungry myself. I'm not quite familiar with this place, but I bet if we look around we could find something to eat."

"Anything would be great by me."

"Let's try to find something to tide us over, perhaps some crackers, or maybe a few cans of soup," Mrs. Ford said in a motherly tone of voice while she put on a robe over her nightgown.

"That works for me." Cassie halfheartedly laughed.

"How are they holding out?"

"Like boys."

"I know where the kitchen is located. That's a start."

"Should I tell them?"

"Boys are pretty noisy creatures," she said, looking Cassie directly in the eyes. "Maybe we should just leave them out of this until there's something solid to report."

Cassie was beginning to feel better. She enjoyed the camaraderie that Mrs. Ford offered. Being together with her brother and a bunch of other guys was fun for the most part, but for now she wanted some female companionship.

Cassie and Mrs. Ford made their way down the long hall and through a massive kitchen doorway. It was immaculate. Everything from canned goods to fresh produce had its place. Even the chrome on the refrigerator was sparkling bright.

Mrs. Ford turned on the lights. Every evil dream and happening that took place over the last 48 hours disappeared at once. She wanted to tell Mrs. Ford everything: the soundless dream on the plane, the shadow man and his horrible smell, the touch that she could still feel on her lips, but there was no way anyone would understand. Cassie wasn't sure if she understood. And what's worse, she wondered if perhaps she was losing her mind.

Just forget it, she thought. For now, just forget about it all. Whatever the future held, it wasn't something that some hummus couldn't solve, or a nice croissant, or maybe even a bagel and lox.

Mrs. Ford started rummaging through the colossal refrigerator, pulling out bits of this and that. She was on a mission and Cassie was there to see the mission through.

"Do you think we should leave the boys out of this?"

Mrs. Ford smiled. "You already asked that Cassie. The answer is— for now, yes." They both started laughing. "If we start to feel guilty for eating all the food, then and only then will we let them in on it, but for now, let's get crazy."

It wasn't long before the two were stuffed to the gills. After a few moments of silence, Cassie, again, wondered if she should talk to Mrs. Ford about what was going on, about her dreams. She admired Mrs. Ford in so many ways, and now she felt close enough to her that she could open up and discuss certain things, certain things that scared the hell out of her. However, the boogeyman was a hard subject to broach with anyone.

"Mrs. Ford, I have a question to ask." Cassie fell silent.

"This sounds serious," said Mrs. Ford, while stuffing her face with peanut butter and crackers.

"First, I just want to tell you that what I'm about to say was probably just a strange dream. The problem I'm having is that sometimes the dream seems awfully real." Cassie waited for a response, desperately wanting to tell Mrs. Ford everything, but at the same time nervous about what she would think.

"I'm all ears, sweetheart."

"Okay... well... Mrs. Ford, do you believe in ghosts?" Cassie stared into her lap.

"I do," said Mrs. Ford without having to think about it. "I believe there are a lot of things that we as people don't understand and refuse to acknowledge. I guess ghosts would fall under that category."

Cassie looked up. Her face must have given away more than she intended, considering how quick Mrs. Ford's response was.

"Did something happen, Cassie?" Mrs. Ford pulled her chair closer, putting her hands on Cassie's shoulders.

"It started happening after my father died. It started with strange dreams. They are the kind of dreams that you remember as if they were real." Cassie stopped, deep in thought.

Mrs. Ford not knowing what was coming next, and not wanting to push Cassie too hard to get there, listened intently, keeping her eyes focused on Cassie's eyes.

Cassie continued. "I saw something, but it wasn't a ghost... so to speak. He was tall, really tall, and dark, darker than the dark itself. His hands and arms were so long, and he had this strange smell to him. Actually, the strangest, worst thing I've ever smelled in my life." Cassie started playing with the plate of food in front of her. She wanted to talk; she wanted to say everything, but once she said it out loud, she realized just how stupid it all sounded.

"Look, Cassie. I'm here to listen. I'm not here to force you to say anything you don't want to. But I've always found it best to talk things out if at all possible."

Cassie took a deep breath and looked up towards the ceiling. There were tiny little stars painted against a blue backdrop.

"Here comes the boogeyman."

"He's got bad breath."

"He's going to get you, sweet-pea."

"He came to the room tonight. The only reason I knew that it was real was that when the boys woke up they could smell him. It was the same smell he always brought." Cassie started to cry. She hated herself for breaking down. Somehow she thought that crying made her look guilty, a liar, a freak, but she knew she was none of these things, or at least she thought she wasn't.

A song started to drift through her head. It was Aerosmith, her father's favorite band singing *Dream on*.

Firmly dismissing the desire to run away, Cassie came back to reality. "How stupid I must sound."

Mrs. Ford wiped Cassie's eyes with a soft touch and smiled understandingly. "Tell you what, Cass. Let's get the guys in here so we can feed them. You and I can talk at length later on. If you want, you can stay in my room. It will be just us girls. I think it would be good for both of us."

Cassie just nodded, unable to meet Mrs. Ford's eyes. Cassie wondered whether any good could come from this at all because of what the man might do to Mrs. Ford.

That night passed without further incident. Cassie slept in Mrs. Ford's room and the next morning she felt better than she ever had in all her life. It was her first official day in Israel. She couldn't wait to see all those things she had only read about; replacing dreams of a man made of shadows for the history of a man made of light.

CHAPTER 5 - THE PLACE OF A SKULL

Mrs. Ford needed some air. There was something heavy upon her and the candles cast shadows in darkness that moved with ferocious speed, faster than her eyes could follow. She told herself to just look away and ignore them, that they were only shadows, that candlelight flickers and tricks the mind into believe something is there that isn't, but she had to look. She had to know. She did not feel like herself at all.

Once she was outside the main entrance of the church, she felt much better, despite the heat from the sun high in the afternoon sky. Standing near the wall, Mrs. Ford leaned forward with her hands on her knees and took deep breaths until her head cleared. For some reason, the feeling reminded her of something from her childhood. Her father died when she was only four and though she couldn't remember anything about her father himself, she could remember everything about his funeral. The usual oppressive heat of New Jersey in July, the way the sunlight glared off the coffin above the grave, her mother's black eyes blurred by tears until she would blink and they would fall.

There were no shadows to sicken her senses back then, but there were the expressions of everyone around her. She remembered standing in front of her mother and looking around at all the eyes looking back at her and feeling something strange in the way they looked at her. Their eyes looked as if they knew something she didn't, as if they were mad at her, as if it was all her fault. She remembered feeling scared and suffocated, and that if her mother wasn't holding her by the shoulders, she would have sunk, or screamed, or both. That was how she felt in the church and that was why there were tears in her eyes now that she felt better.

It was the sound of a small boy that brought her back to her senses and lifted her head. A white handkerchief was being held out to her. Behind the handkerchief were large brown eyes, a round face and a mess of wispy black hair. In his other hand, the boy held a large, brown, leather-bound book. "Missus?" the boy kept saying, concerned and curious with a tilt of his head.

"Thank you," Mrs. Ford said with a grateful smile on her face, taking the handkerchief from him to dry her eyes and closing them while doing so. When she opened them again once she was done, the little boy was gone. Mrs. Ford scanned her surroundings, but there was no sign of him at all. "How strange," she said to herself.

Before she could consider her strange encounter the group was exiting the church, led by Cassie who was demonstratively speaking with her hands to Frankie and Max. Both boys were nodding their heads as if they were hearing something they've heard a million times before.

Mrs. Ford stuffed the handkerchief in her pocket and straightened herself out as the group approached. Frankie with a look of utter frustration was the first to address her.

"Mrs. Ford," he began, "I hope you're feeling better because my sister won't shut up."

Cassie, who had been in the middle of expounding on how cool it was that Adam and Jesus might be buried in the same place, upon hearing Frankie, immediately shut up to punch her brother in the arm and say, "You shut up!"

Frankie punched her back and said, "How can I even have the chance to shut up if you won't shut up!"

Cassie knitted her brows. "What does that even mean?"

"Enough you two," Mrs. Ford finally interjected, having to hide a smile while doing so. "Come on, everyone," she announced to all of them, "we only have a couple of hours left for sightseeing before we have to get to the library to do our research for the dig. Let's get some lunch and then we can head over to the Dome of the Rock if we have time."

Mrs. Ford's announcement was met with only silence. Kyle and Ryan were busy staring at a man in white robes leading a camel. Frankie and Cassie were busy staring at each other, occasionally feigning punches. Max was marveling at just how much sweat he was capable of producing. Mrs. Ford clapped her hands once in the air and said in a slightly sterner voice, "I need everybody to listen to me now!"

Five sets of wide eyes turned to her.

"That's better," she said. "Now everybody pair up—Max you're with me—and let's get something to eat."

The five of them sighed, but they followed nonetheless, leaving behind the Church of the Holy Sepulcher for a falafel stand.

Mrs. Ford went to order the falafels while the group gathered at the tables outside. Cassie, still lost in thought over the morning's events, chose a table of her own. The four boys took turns asking her if it was because they smelled bad, which eventually evolved into a series of fart jokes, before they sat at a table themselves.

Cassie had no patience for such nonsense. That morning she had been in the very place where Christ was crucified. Things that she had only read about, things that she had only dreamt about came to life before her eyes like she could never have imagined possible. Not only could she feel the place, but the place felt her. And as she stood there among the candles and the shadows and the sounds of reverence and awe, she thought of Him and all she wanted to do was cry.

"Because He knew who He was," she said to herself while looking down at her hands, feeling the sadness fill her body again, "and He knew what He had to do."

"You think?" spoke a voice from nearby.

Cassie looked up to see an old, wrinkled man sitting at the table in front of her. The old man looked at her with a kind smile. He had a small face, but all the wrinkles and the Panama hat on his head made it seem fuller.

Cassie was not used to random old men speaking to her, so she stared back with her mouth slightly opened.

"What I think," the man thoughtfully began, "is that we know because He knows." The man pointed up without looking up when he said 'He'. Then he nodded his head. "He tells us what we should do and if we listen, we hear. Do you know what he told me to do?"

Cassie tilted her head with curiosity. "No, what?" she asked.

"He told me to get cable TV, so I get cable TV, and I don't even like TV, but now I have cable TV."

Cassie wanted to laugh out loud but she wasn't sure if the man was joking or not, so she was careful to laugh to herself. She was still laughing when she said, "I'm not sure I believe in..."

"What, cable? Oh, believe me, little Miss, it is true and I have over four hundred channels to prove it," the man said, his smile expanding into his wrinkles.

Cassie did laugh out loud this time. "No, I meant..."

"I know what you meant," the man interrupted. "Nobody believes in cable TV anymore. Not much sure if I do either. But what I do know is that when God told Noah to build an ark, he built an ark. And when God told Moses to climb a mountain, he climbed a mountain. And when God told Jesus that He was His son, he became His son, and God, His father." The old man stopped speaking but his jaw continued moving, as if he was chewing on something. His eyes glazed over lost in thought. After a moment like this, he blinked and looked back up at Cassie. "And what did God say to you?"

Cassie thought it over for a second. Then she said with a nod of her head, "I think God told me to come to Israel."

The old man smiled even wider than before. "I think he told you more than that, little lady."

Cassie could hear Mrs. Ford bringing the food to the boy's table and she turned to see her place the tray in the middle of it, which was immediately descended upon by the boys. When she turned back around, the old man was already standing.

"And now if you'll excuse me," he said, "I think God is telling me that Iron Chef is on. I really love that show." The man smiled at Cassie one last time. Then he said goodbye and left.

Cassie said goodbye too with a wave and then she watched him slowly walk away. "I don't even know what his name was," she said to herself as Mrs. Ford sat down next to her with another tray of food.

"Who, honey?" Mrs. Ford asked.

Cassie turned to Mrs. Ford and sighed. "Nobody," she said. Then she ate falafel and told Mrs. Ford all about the Place of the Skull.

Later that night, Cassie woke to a familiar sound; faint, unpredictable and unusual. It was hushed, barely a whisper. It was there. She strained her eyes in the dark to see.

In the dim light she could see Mrs. Ford was fast asleep. She could hear her snoring away loud enough that it should have blocked out any other sound in the room.

And then, suddenly, he was there. She knew he was aware of her knowing and she froze. Any moment a scream would escape her lips. Cassie pulled the covers up over her face, exposing only her eyes. The stench caused them to burn. She knew nothing mattered. She knew that something was going to happen tonight.

She had to face this.

"Who are you?" she whispered. Cassie pushed herself deeper into the bed, trying to disappear within the matting.

He was standing near her now, hovering, waiting for more words so that he could touch her, reach down her throat and rip out her soul. Her lips felt numb as she anticipated his touch and the pain she had felt just the night before.

From the boy's room next door the sound of terror filtered through the walls. Her secret was out. Whatever or whoever this shadow man was, he had now included the rest of the group. Mrs. Ford woke up and clicked on the light. Her eyes went wide with horror.

"Cassie we need to leave immediately," she said.

Cassie looked around for the shadow man but he was nowhere to be seen. The horrible odor still lingered but the thing that produced it was gone. Mrs. Ford was already grabbing her things at breakneck speed and Cassie, realizing the panic in the way she moved, jumped out of bed and started doing the same. It seemed they had all figured it out. Cassie's dream was no dream.

It was real.

And they were leaving.

"I want everybody in the lobby now!" cried Mrs. Ford with such force that it sent chills down Cassie's spine. The rest of the youth hostel was awake now. If it wasn't the shadow men, it was the sickeningly smell of Meat Incense.

"What the hell is going on here?" said one of the professors, as he swiftly put on a robe as he came out of his room.

"Professor Brown, we need to get everybody out of here now!" Mrs. Ford looked at him with such dread that he did not hesitate, and he started rounding up his own group of students.

The door to the hostel was locked every evening at eight o'clock, but tonight somebody was there, unlocking the door event though it was three in the morning. It was a boy. He was no more than ten. He had the keys and a strange book in his hand; it was a book Cassie and Frankie knew immediately and their hearts sank in fear and wonder. It was their father's journal. And the boy, this smallish, waif of a boy with wispy black hair and dark brown eyes, knew who they were. He called to them by name.

The rush of reality was too much for Cassie to bear. She glanced at Mrs. Ford and then Frank as they moved towards the boy and the open door. Frankie's face was pale. He looked scared.

"Most of my people stay at the site," said Professor Brown. "I think we should all assemble there."

"I'm sorry," said Mrs. Ford as she ushered the last of her group out the door.

Max looked at Cassie and Frank. "Sorry? What's she sorry for?" But before either of them could consider the question, they were all outside and the little boy who had unlocked the door was gone.

Cassie looked up into the darkness of the Jerusalem night. Then she looked back down at Frankie. Frankie's face still looked white no matter how dark it was. Voices mumbled all around them, but the silence between them was heavy with fear and uncertainty. She waited for Frankie to say something, to say anything, but he only stood there shaking his head and looking back at her with his mouth slightly opened.

Finally, with tears in her eyes, Cassie pushed her brother in his chest with both hands and said, louder than she intended, "What are we going to do now?"

Frankie wanted to give his sister a hug. Frankie wanted to tell her that everything was going to be alright. But instead he just shook his head and said, "I don't know."

It was not the answer Cassie was looking for.

CHAPTER 6 - STEEL ON STONE

The streets of the Old City were dark and narrow, and they all seemed to lead to nothing but more darkness. Panicked muttering turned to silence once the last student had made it out of the hostel. It was as if they realized how strange and how dangerous a situation they were in all at the same time. Once the silence set in, it only seemed stranger and darker, and narrow streets that lead to nothing seemed to hold something far more sinister than just more darkness.

"But there are no shadows in the darkness," Cassie told herself, though even she didn't believe it at this point. A part of her wanted to feel better. The man that had been haunting her ever since her father's death, emerging from her dreams and into her reality, had finally been confirmed. She was not crazy, not at all. But another part of her felt like something had been lost, something she would never get back again. It scared her and saddened her because she knew it was too late to stop now, no matter what may be awaiting her in the darkness around the corner, and no matter what she may lose of herself next.

Mrs. Ford and Professor Brown stood at the front of the group, whispering to each other. The rest of the students tried to keep their focus on them but they were all still rattled from the events of the night. They couldn't help nervously looking all around, especially since they were not moving away from the hostel which was filled with unexplainable, smelly men. Frank was searching intently for the boy with his father's journal, though he was nowhere to be found. Max was biting his nails. Cassie was trying to imagine she wasn't hearing what she was hearing.

It sounded like steel scraping slowly over stone, and it sounded like it was far away, down the street in the darkness. Cassie looked around to see if anyone else noticed it, but nobody else seemed to. She stared in the direction of the sound. She held her breath. And there it was again. And it seemed to be getting closer.

Cassie clenched her jaw. Cassie tried to stop tears from coming to her eyes. She wondered if it was real. She wondered if the whole world was against her. She wanted to tell Mrs. Ford. She wanted to scream. But she was afraid that if it wasn't real and she told somebody about it, that it would become real, just like with the shadow man. But if it was real and she didn't tell anybody, they would all find out what was making that horrible sound. She didn't know what to do. She didn't know what to think. So she clenched her jaw tighter and tears came to her eyes and the sound of steel on stone only got louder.

"Um, Mrs. Ford?" Cassie let out meekly.

Mrs. Ford seemed to be arguing with Professor Brown while trying not to seem like they were arguing. Both of them were well aware that they did not know the streets of Jerusalem as well as they should, especially in the middle of the night. Upon hearing Cassie's voice, Mrs. Ford looked in her direction, her expression strained and her eyes red. "What is it, Cassie?" she said, trying to hide the panic in her voice.

Cassie furrowed her brows. She didn't know how to say what she needed to say without coming out and saying it. She looked behind her toward the terrible scraping sound that was quickly approaching. Any minute whatever was making it would be standing before them all. She turned back around to Mrs. Ford and said with her chin trembling, "I think we should go now."

Mrs. Ford's expression changed completely. Strain, fear, and panic immediately washed away and was replaced with an expression of urgency. She nodded her head and smiled, a smile meant only for Cassie. "All right," she announced to the group, "everybody stay close and follow me." Then she turned to face the darkness, took a deep breath and started walking.

The students moved in silence, which to Cassie was worse than the scraping. Scuffling shoes upon sandstone echoed through the narrow streets of the Old City and everywhere she looked Cassie expected to see a man made of shadows holding a shovel and running it slowly along the wall while he smiled back at her. Occasionally she thought she could hear it, far off from some distant street, following her, the way the moon seems to follow you no matter where you go.

Mrs. Ford led the way. Professor Brown was at the back of the group. In between the adults, whenever Cassie would think she heard it, she would look for the back of Mrs. Ford's head to the face of Professor Brown for reassurance. Frankie was at one side of her, and Max at the other. None of them said a word the entire time, but the looks they exchanged spoke volumes. Frank was obviously frightened; his muscles tensed. Cassie could tell what Frankie was thinking. Someone or something was after his sister and that he would protect her no matter what it took. Max seemed frightened in a different way. He was more worried than prepared and when he would turn to Cassie, she could see something else in his eyes, and she wondered if he would look that way if he were looking at Frankie instead of her.

They turned one corner and then another. There were no lights on these streets, just an occasional dull bulb high on a wall, but otherwise just moonlight. It seemed like they were walking forever, trapped in a maze, but finally they reached a narrow street that led to a larger one. A streetlamp came into view and a collective sigh of relief rose from the group. All they had to do was reach it and they'd be safe, at least from the darkness. Just one more, long, narrow street lay between the streets of darkness and the relief of light and other people. But then a figure passed slowly past the end, momentarily taking them back into darkness. Again, at the end of the street the blur of a body passing in front of the light was unidentifiable from the distance. And then there was another.

Mrs. Ford looked behind her to Professor Brown. The group could see her breathing harder, faster. She had a curious expression, as if she was asking a question without asking it.

Professor Brown simply shook his head at her and then shrugged. So, Mrs. Ford turned back around, took a deep breath and continued on.

Finally they reached the street and the lamplight. Mrs. Ford had slowed her approach, and the group's, the closer they got. But there they were, in the light, and that's when Mrs. Ford stopped and let out a startled breath and stared off to her side.

The group turned their heads to see what she was looking at. It was a bench beneath a streetlight and seated on the bench was an old man with a brown paper bag opened on his lap. The man did not seem to notice them. Instead he was staring at the ground in front of him, his face pale and expressionless beneath the light, his movement slow and deliberate as if he was not in control of what he was doing.

The man was slowly removing something from the bag, something that he held in a closed hand, which he then threw onto the ground. It looked like birdseed, but there were no birds. And yet he wouldn't stop. A hand slowly emptied would soon be a hand slowly filled.

Mrs. Ford recovered quickly and turned around again to the group with a hand on her chest. She seemed as if she wasn't sure if she should scream, or if she should laugh. So she just shrugged and started walking again. What none of them had noticed until they started walking again, passing the old man from the other side of the street, was the old woman standing next to the bench. Cassie saw her first; maybe because the woman was staring right at her.

The woman wore the same expressionless face, but when Cassie's and the woman's eyes met, something changed. Her eyes seemed to open wider, and then slowly, like the motion of the man, her lips began to stretch, until eventually, finally, she was smiling, but it was like no smile Cassie had ever seen before. The old woman didn't have any teeth, but she was smiling as if she did, and where they should have been, was the blackest, darkest space Cassie had ever seen.

"But there are no shadows in the darkness," Cassie said to herself again. Then the sound came again. Steel on stone as if it was all around them, and everybody turned their heads to listen.

Mrs. Ford didn't have to turn around to look at Professor Brown before she realized what was happening. She knew this was not right and she immediately started moving faster. First at a highly accelerated walk, until the sound grew even louder and they were running. Darkness and light like black and white pages of a book turning faster and faster until it was all a blur, and the sound of breathing beneath the sound of steel scraping against stone walls, as everything happened at once, and running through the night, through streetlights and darkness, one final light appeared before them, and they stopped.

It was the library where they had been doing their research and Mrs. Ford recognized it at once. The sound subsided but then started again as Mrs. Ford tried the door, which was, of course, locked. Looking back, Cassie, Frank and Max could see the old man sitting at the bench, still throwing seed onto the street. Mrs. Ford and a small group of students closest to her wrestled with the door but to no avail.

Frank said, "What the hell is going on?"

Max watched as small creatures began to emerge from dark places around the old man on the bench, scurrying to the seeds to sit and gnaw on them. "Why the hell is he feeding the rats?" he said.

Cassie looked all around for the source of the sound, the shadow man with the shovel, but saw nothing as the sound rose again.

"Because God told him to feed rats," she said to Max, looking around the corner of the library. A window was cracked, and the wind scraped through it sounding like steel. "There!" she exclaimed.

Professor Brown saw where she was pointing and rushed to the window to crack it open with his elbow, cutting himself in the process. Blood dripped from a broken edge as he reached inside to open it, climbing in once it was.

"How do you know what God told him?" Max asked Cassie as Professor Brown opened the library door from the inside.

Cassie didn't have time to answer him as the group ran into the safety of the library, but before the door closed, she was able to look back and saw the old woman walking slowly towards her, stopping in the midst of the rats eating seed. And then the door closed. And the darkness was different. The silence was too simple to be soundless.

CHAPTER 7 - CASSIE'S BEST WORK

After being in the dark for so long, the bright lights of the library were a shock to all of them. It seemed like a lifetime since they had been indoors and the relief was obvious on all of their faces. A collective sigh broke the silence as they all slowly sat down at the tables, followed by mumbling as the group began to recall the incredible events of that night. Mrs. Ford and Professor Brown were the only ones to not sit down yet. They were too busy whispering to each other. Mrs. Ford was speaking with her hands as Professor Brown just listened and nodded.

Cassie, Frankie, and Max did not know what to say to each other. They sat down at one end of a table, staring first at their laps and then their hands and finally into each other's expressionless faces. It was Max who finally broke the silence.

"Well, that just happened," he said.

"You can say that again," Frankie agreed.

Cassie just sat there in stunned silence. That terrible sound in her ears, that putridly sweet smell of death, it was all too much to handle. She didn't even notice it when Mrs. Ford sat down next to her, nor did she hear a word that was spoken to her. Mrs. Ford had to gently shake her by the shoulder in order to get her attention.

Finally, she looked up to hear Mrs. Ford say, "Cassie, dear, is that what you were talking about?"

Cassie looked down at her hands embarrassed, as if everything that was happening was her fault. "It is, and I'm sorry I didn't say anything earlier. I tried but…"

Mrs. Ford was shaken. Her entire life was spent being curious about things like this, but tonight; tonight was real. She rubbed Cassie's shoulders to try to encourage her to continue. Cassie did, but was still unable to look Mrs. Ford in the eyes.

"I should've said something, I know, but how do you explain something like this? How do you know you're not just going crazy? I mean I really tried. It's just… just…" Cassie took a deep breath. She felt spent, and trying to explain it all made her to feel more grief than fear. "Like I told you earlier, it all started with my dreams."

Mrs. Ford moved her hand to the back of Cassie's head, knowing how hard it must be for her to talk about it. "You can talk to me, dear," she said as she tried to comfort Cassie by stroking her hair. "It'll make you feel better. When did the dreams first start?"

Cassie did feel better and she finally turned to Mrs. Ford. The tears in her eyes were unavoidable but she tried to steady her voice as she spoke. "After my father… you know… after he died, Frankie seemed to be okay and all, although I know he was hurting. He never complained about anything. He tried to be strong. I think he was doing it for me, because it was almost like losing our mom too. She didn't know how to deal with it at all. It was like she was just lost in the sadness."

Tears came to Mrs. Ford's eyes too, but she didn't wipe them away. "I'm sorry," she said after gulping down the lump in her throat.

"She's better now," Cassie said reassuringly.

"And that's when the dreams started?" Mrs. Ford asked.

Cassie looked down again and nodded her head.

"I've never seen anything like this," said Mrs. Ford. "And I have to admit Cassie, I'm afraid as well. But I just can't see how your father's death relates to this, this thing, or should I say these things." Mrs. Ford looked down at her own hands and took a deep breath. "I've lost loved ones before. My grandfather passed away less than two years ago, and I had some bad dreams about it, but this is something different altogether."

"At least I know now I'm not going crazy," said Cassie. She folded her arms and shivered as if she were cold.

Frank had been pretending not to listen, but now that there was a break in the conversation, he finally put a voice to his thoughts. For all the years of their lives, Cassie had never kept one secret from him, not one. Not until now, he thought.

"Cassie this is getting stupid," he started. "You've been acting crazy ever since dad's death. It was hard on me too, you know. But then you became all different, treating everyone like an outsider, even me. Well... it just hurts." Frank was not one to talk about how he felt often, so he was not used to it. He picked up a magazine on the table in front of him and pretended to read. It was written in Hebrew. Hebrew was a language he'd never even seen before, let alone read.

"I'm sorry," offered Cassie.

"You're sorry?" Frankie answered angrily. "You're sorry for what, Cassie? For leaving me out of your life as if you were the only one in pain? For letting me deal with dad's death alone? For letting you deal with these dreams alone?" Frankie slammed the magazine down on the table. The noise it made was enough to catch everyone else's attention. He hadn't intended on creating drama. What happened tonight wasn't the issue, at least not for him. What he saw certainly scared him, but the way his twin sister was treating him, like some stranger, was far scarier than any dream, real or otherwise.

"Frank, I'm sorry. I can't tell you how sorry I am. I never meant to... it's just... it's just that I didn't want to blow this whole thing out of proportion. At first I thought it was only happening to me, you know, like as if I was going crazy or something." Cassie started to cry. She couldn't keep it inside any longer.

Mrs. Ford looked on in silence at the two of them. She knew this was something they had to work out between them, as only a brother and sister could. She wanted to comfort Cassie. She wanted to tell Frankie that it wasn't Cassie's fault. But she didn't. She just listened with her hand on Cassie's back for support.

Frankie could see how much pain his sister was in and felt even worse than before for contributing to it. "I'm sorry too," he said. He hated it when she cried.

Cassie looked up, her eyes red from tears. She forced a smile. Gazing upon her concerned brother's face made her feel stronger.

Frankie forced a smile back, but held back his own tears.

Mrs. Ford nodded her head. She knew how meaningful such a thing was from brother and sister. But now there was the even more difficult task of preparing the rest of the group for what lay ahead. She loudly cleared her throat and waved for everybody to gather around the table. She wasn't exactly sure what she was going to say, but one thing was certain, she wasn't going to lie.

Ryan, Kyle and the rest of the students quickly made their way to the table. They didn't seem scared anymore. In fact, from what Mrs. Ford could tell, they now seemed excited.

"If you guys have answers, please share," said Ryan. The rest agreed.

"This is a tough one," said Mrs. Ford.

"I have something I want to tell you guys," started Cassie, "and I don't want you to be mad at me." The group stared back at her with curious expressions. "Okay… well… and remember, don't be mad at me, but…"

Then, without apparent reason, the lights flickered twice and faded out. Everyone froze. Cassie felt a chill straight away. She looked at the others and in the dim light, while questioning eyes looked back at her.

Cassie wanted to say something. She wanted to assure them that she had nothing to do with this. She wanted to be able to explain what was happening. She wanted to have all the answers. Yes, it started with her. But now, everyone played a part. The rules were simple. No one had a say in what was happening and no one could make it stop, not even her.

She opened her mouth to speak but before she could, she heard something overhead. It sounded like the flutter of wings. All of them could hear it and as one, they slowly looked up.

Something else flew overhead but it moved too fast to see what it was, then another, and then another, until the entire space above their heads seemed to be swarming with them. Someone let out a high-pitched shriek. They all looked down expecting it to be Cassie or one of the other girls, but it was Ryan. He was covering his mouth with both his hands and when he saw everybody looking at him, he removed them to say, "I hate bats."

Another shriek came from one of the boys, followed by another, as they all quickly looked up again to get a good look at them. Apparently, they all hated bats.

"I don't think they're bats," Mrs. Ford said. "I think they're books."

It was at that moment that one of them flew lower, grazing the side of Kyle's head.

"You're right!" he said.

Without any of them having to be told, they all immediately dropped to the ground and crawled for safety underneath the sturdy oak table.

"What the fff—" Max began stuttering before being stopped by Mrs. Ford with a "Max!"

"Sorry, Mrs. Ford," he said.

Frank, however, focused his attention on his sister. "Cassie, what the hell is going on?" he asked, accusingly.

She was about to tell him that she had no idea what was going on, that there was no possible way she could know what was going on. She was about to apologize again for dragging them all into this, especially her own brother. But just as she opened her mouth, she saw something in the far corner of the library, something that made her forget everything she was about to say and something that made everybody turn to see what she was looking at.

It was a man, a man dressed all in black, but somehow different from the other men they had seen. He was sitting on a small rug with his legs crossed. Below his top hat, they all watched as a flame was lit, alighting his eyes and a wicked smile that played across his face. The flame was extinguished to reveal a cigarette, and the smoke that was exhaled, curled and swirled like a snake in a shallow stream.

Mrs. Ford who was more frightened than ever, caught a flash of mischievousness in the creature's eyes. She was stunned by the hatred she also saw there.

The brooding hum of at least twenty men chanting filtered its way through the room, circling with tedious resolve, making the space even more repressive and repulsive. The dark man looked across at them. He had so skillfully mastered their awareness. He took them away with just a glance. He stood up, and closing his eyes, placed his hands upon a large book that sat singularly atop a small tea table. He looked enraptured, as though he wanted to capture the moment forever.

"It's your best work, Cassie. The best thing I've ever read of yours," he said in a whisper that somehow carried through the chanting all the way from the other side of the room. "Hopefully this will ensure you a place at the top of the mountain. Hopefully I will finally be able to impress upon you the nature of your work, the reason why you're here. You are a succulent little creature, you and that smug, little brother of yours."

Cassie was more confused than frightened. How did this man

know her name? What work was he talking about? And why was he talking to her like he already knew her? She looked apprehensively at the others, as they were all still huddled underneath the long wooden table. Except for Frank, Max and Mrs. Ford, the rest of them had separated themselves from her.

The man held his gaze and looked at her in wonder through the thin grey clouds of smoke that swirled aimlessly around her head. "You don't understand your purpose, do you? Have you forgotten everything your father taught you? Or are you still hoping that this is all but a dream?" The dark man started to laugh an unnatural laugh and all the books still on the shelves and all the books fluttering like bats through the air, began to fall to the ground as if the cadence of the man's voice carried something solid and deadly.

It sounded like the whole world was crashing down all around them, but something was happening inside of Cassie. She was angry, very angry and most definitely not afraid. It was one thing for this man to say things about her, but it was quite another when it was her father.

She crawled out from beneath the table and stood up. The shadow man stopped laughing. The corners of his mouth curled until his smile became a sneer and his teeth gleamed unnaturally white, the ends jagged like that of a shark's. He brought his shoulders back, standing up to his full height, his head now but a foot below the ceiling. And yet, Cassie stood her ground.

"We're leaving this place," said Cassie, calmly and confidently. "We're leaving this place now."

As if on cue, powered by Cassie's bravery, Mrs. Ford and the rest of the group made a beeline for the front door. Cassie followed. She was the last one to leave but she looked back just before closing the door. The man was gone. All of the books were back neatly on the shelves. It was as if no one had been there at all. Cassie smiled, nodded her head and slammed the door.

CHAPTER 8 - BIG MAN, PIG MAN

Morning and pale yellow sunlight fell over tall grey buildings, as they all gathered in the street leading to the library. No more shadows, no more bats made of books, nobody sitting at benches feeding rats, just deep breaths of fresh air and tired eyes, red from being roughly rubbed free of their dreams.

Cassie was the last to join them, walking tiredly down the street with her shoulders slumped and her head down. She felt a power and a confidence she had never felt before, which felt good. But she would have easily given up such a feeling if it meant never having to go through what she just went through, especially since it also involved all the people she liked and loved.

Frank was the first to greet her, hugging her even though she didn't have the strength to hug him back. He let go of her and looked as if he was going to say something, but nothing came out. Instead he just shook his head and hugged her again. This time she managed to lift an arm to hug him back.

Max looked on with a dry smile on his face. "I told you libraries were evil," he said when Frank let her go the second time.

Cassie snorted slightly, which was the most laughter she could manage at this point. "I guess you can now include hostels, old men and bird-feeding in that category too."

Max smiled and nodded in agreement, but before he could say something else, Professor Brown interrupted him. He seemed to be the most rattled of the group and immediately began demanding that Cassie tell him why this was happening and what was happening and how she could drag them all into this thing with her, as well as a whole host of other unanswerable questions.

Cassie, who was in no mood to be accused of such things, steeled her gaze upon him, and as her mouth opened to use words she had never said to an adult before, not to their face at least, Mrs. Ford came to her defense.

"Lester!" she said, taking him by the arm and turning him towards her. "Leave the poor girl alone! She's already been through enough tonight and she doesn't need you making it worse."

Professor Brown stared back at Mrs. Ford for a moment with his mouth open in surprise, but quickly recovered. He apologized to Cassie even though he was unable to look her in the eyes while he did. Then he took his position at the back of the group, still shaking his head as he did.

Mrs. Ford continued to stare at him, just in case he had anything else to say. "And I want you all to know," she said to the group, "none of this is Cassie's fault. Whatever is happening has a logical explanation and we will figure it out together. We will all get through this *together*."

Mrs. Ford's announcement was met with silence, which was finally broken by Max. "So where do we go now? Are there some haunted sewers we can check out while we're here?"

Mrs. Ford laughed, more out of relief than anything else.

"I've always wanted to surf Loch Ness," Kyle added.

Ryan turned red for his turn. "Think it's supposed to be a full moon tonight. I can see it now, Cassie Lint starring in the blockbuster new movie 'Dances with Werewolves'."

Everybody laughed except for Frank, who seemed lost in thought.

Max noticed this and put his hand on Frank's shoulder. "Don't worry, Frankie," he said. "I think we can find a part for you in 'Bravefart'."

This worked for the moment, and Frank relaxed and laughed too. Normally Mrs. Ford would not encourage such humor, but given everything they had been through, she needed to laugh as much as everybody else and to everybody's surprise she was laughing harder than anyone else.

Finally she returned to her senses and made the announcement that their next stop was not, in fact, haunted sewers but the American Embassy. "Seems it's the only place left we have to go," she said.

"Think I'd rather deal with farting sewer werewolves than some politicians," Max mumbled to himself.

"Unfortunately, Max," Mrs. Ford said with a laugh, "they're pretty much one and the same."

Max laughed too, suddenly appreciating Mrs. Ford more than ever.

Mrs. Ford took a deep breath, told everybody to stay close to one another, and then they all started the long walk for the embassy.

Everything that happened the night before seemed even more unreal in the reality of a new day. The Old City had never looked more beautiful than the way it looked that morning. And though they were all exhausted, they were happy and relaxed, and there was a collective feeling that soon there would be an answer to all the strange things that happened to them. Even Cassie could feel it. The sun was so warm and the day so beautiful. *"How could such dark things exist in a world that was capable of such light,"* she thought.

Mrs. Ford, however, did not seem to have the same reaction. The closer they got to the embassy, the more nervous she seemed to become.

Finally, they neared the entrance to the Embassy. There was a basketball court at the far end of the courtyard and Mrs. Ford instructed Professor Brown to wait there with the group. Mrs. Ford held Cassie back, telling her that she needed to talk to her. Cassie had been expecting such a thing, but she was certainly not looking forward to it. Neither was Mrs. Ford.

"Cassie," she began, "I really need... I mean, if you could... I mean, if you can." Mrs. Ford took a deep breath through her nose. She looked down at Cassie with a serious expression and tried again. "Cassie, I want you to explain to me why you think this is happening. I know it's hard but I need you to do your best. To be quite honest I don't know how I'm going to explain this to the Embassy without sounding completely..." She stopped herself, not wanting to confirm what Cassie was already afraid would happen. She shook her head and said, more to herself than to Cassie, "I'm really thinking we should just leave."

71

"That would probably be best," replied Cassie.

"No one is blaming you, sweetheart."

"Everyone's blaming me, Mrs. Ford. That's the problem. I really truly don't know what's going on." Cassie looked down at her hands, feeling guilty and embarrassed.

Mrs. Ford sighed and tried again. "Well," she began, "is there any connection between this place and you, maybe with some relatives, or your parents even? Didn't you say the dreams started after your father died?"

Cassie nodded her head and looked up. "They did, but doesn't everybody have bad dreams after something horrible happens?"

"I'm sure they do," Mrs. Ford said calmly, "but not everybody has them come true. What did your father do?"

Cassie looked down again. "We never really talked about it. He was into research or something." She took a deep breath, suddenly realizing a connection that she didn't want to admit to.

Mrs. Ford could sense this and put her hand on Cassie's shoulder. "Is there something else that you're not telling me, Cassie?"

Cassie swallowed hard. She was afraid to say what she was about to say. She was afraid of losing her only ally beside Frankie and Max.

"It's okay," Mrs. Ford reassured her. "Whatever it is, it's okay."

Cassie swallowed again, but she didn't look up when she spoke. "His research... It was here in Jerusalem. I thought... I mean, I hoped... I don't know." When she finally did look up there were tears in her eyes. "I thought that if I came here I could get to know him a little better, you know? He was gone so much of our lives, I just thought... It's stupid, I know... But I thought it would help explain everything...

Then the dreams and my mom and being so excited... and now..." Cassie couldn't hold it in any longer and brought her hands to her face to cover her tears.

Mrs. Ford only shook her head. She could feel that overwhelming sense of loss she felt when her father passed away. Every concern regarding the night before faded away and the instincts of her good nature took over. She put her arms around Cassie and held her while she cried. After Cassie had shed her last tear, Mrs. Ford kissed her once on the forehead and told her that everything was going to be okay.

For some reason, Cassie actually believed her.

Mrs. Ford smiled. Then she turned and mounted the steps of the Embassy. From the open door, she turned back around to say, "I'll be right back." And then she was gone.

The embassy office was large but well proportioned, considering the amount of people within it. Mrs. Ford counted a total of thirteen at one point, but since they kept entering and exiting the room, it was hard to keep an accurate count. They were all men, which did not surprise Mrs. Ford at all, but what did surprise her was the way they were dressed. Except for the Embassy General, a large piggish man named Jonathan with fleshy eyelids and milky blue eyes, all the men wore black suits, white shirts, pink ties and dark Ray Ban sunglasses. Jonathan, however, wore the same black suit except his tie was a very deep red, reminding Mrs. Ford of an animal's tongue after a feeding. He also was not wearing any sunglasses, though Mrs. Ford suspected that the bulge in his chest beneath his jacket was a pair in his shirt pocket. The smell in the room felt abnormally thick, like wet earth. The atmosphere was heavy. It felt like a swamp and Mrs. Ford was already sweating.

The way the man named Jonathan listened to Mrs. Ford's story, with his thick, moist lips slightly parted, an even slighter curl to the corners of them as if at any moment he would break into a sneer, made her think of the lyrics from one of her favorite Pink Floyd songs: "Big man, Pig man". And the thought of it, made her have to hold back a sneer of her own.

"So let me get this straight," the man named Jonathan began again as he leaned back in his chair and turned his fingers into a steeple, "you took a group of kids out of the safety of a hostel and ushered them through the streets of Jerusalem in the middle of the night." He paused for a moment as if he were praying to the church of his fingers in front of him. He shot a glance to a man in sunglasses standing beside the desk and continued. "You can see why we would find this information a bit...perplexing, and just a trifle odd."

Mrs. Ford never cared much for people who used the word 'trifle' in such a way. She leaned forward uncomfortably in her chair, feeling the sweat run in rivulets down her back. "But you see there were... what I mean to say is that we really had no choice in the matter given the..."

"Extenuating circumstances?" Jonathan interrupted, tilting his head with a look of inner amusement on his face, giving Mrs. Ford the impression that he knew more than he was letting on. "And what, pray tell, were these...extenuating circumstances?"

Mrs. Ford looked nervously down at her hands. She knew there was no way to avoid telling the story, but she had hoped that there would be somebody more understanding to tell it to. The way this man looked at her sent chills down her spine. "Well, it's a little hard to explain," she began.

Jonathan slowly leaned forward in his chair, planting his elbows firmly upon the desk and his chin firmly in his hands. "Try me," he sneered.

Mrs. Ford leaned back in her chair. If not for the fact that they had nowhere else to go, she would have leapt from the chair and run from the building. She opened her mouth to speak, but she was interrupted again with a pointed finger in the air from the piggish man behind the desk in front of her.

"And to make it easier on you, why not just begin with the Lint girl," he said, using that same pointed finger to direct one of the men in the room to the door.

Mrs. Ford heard it lock noisily and definitely behind her, but she did not dare turn around. She did not dare take her eyes off the man named Jonathan in front of her, because the way he was staring at her made her more afraid than she ever had been before in her life. And when the other men in the room began closing the curtains, she knew she would probably never see the light of day again.

CHAPTER 9 - I, KEY

Cassie sat on the ground with her back against the fence. The basketball game continued in front of her; normal things for a normal world. Kyle snagged a rebound, passed the ball to Frank. Frank held the ball for a second at half court while Bernie, a boy in their Pre-Calculus class rushed in front of him with his arms up. Frank gave Bernie a head-fake; then did a crossover dribble to get around him. This time two players from the opposing team hurried to Frank in defense. Frank faked a pass to Ryan before sending a no-look pass to Max. Max was staring at Cassie and the ball bounced perfectly off of his forehead.

"Jesus, Max!" Frank complained, shaking his head with his hands out. "Get your head in the game!"

"I thought it was," Max mumbled while rubbing the red spot on his forehead.

Normally Cassie would find such a thing rather amusing, but at that moment she was too lost in her thoughts to find amusement in anything at all. At that moment, she was filled with unexplainable sadness, which, with everything happening in her life recently, was the last thing she expected to feel. It troubled her even more than what the stranger in the library had said, and as she sat there, she no longer wondered what was happening to her. At that moment, she was more concerned with what was wrong with her. She didn't even notice Max standing next to her with the basketball in his hands.

"Let me guess," he said with a smile on his face, tossing the basketball back to Frankie, "you're wondering what vampires do about daylight savings time."

Cassie remained sullen even as she looked up at Max. "Well, considering they probably sleep in different places, they use their cell phones as an alarm too, and the time would change automatically. So, no, I was not thinking about that."

Max nodded his head in appreciation of her vampire logic. "Yeah, but cell phone stores are only open during the day so how would they be able to set up service."

"Cell phone stores are not only open during the day!" Cassie said annoyed. "Malls are usually open until 10 p.m. Plus you can just do all that stuff over the Internet now anyway." Cassie shook her head before adding: "Duh."

"That is true," Max said impressed.

"Hey, Max! What's up?" Ryan called from across the basketball court.

"Yeah! What's up? Are you in or not?" Kyle added.

"In a second!" Max yelled. Without taking his attention from Cassie he sat down next to her close enough so that their knees would touch should either of them shift weight.

"So what were you thinking about?" he asked. "What the guy in the library said?"

Cassie still looked down at her hands, still with the weight of sadness on her chest. She just shook her head instead of answering.

"Is it those smelly, shadowy guys?" he tried.

"Nope," Cassie answered simply.

"Um… Is it maybe about how I got so awesome in basketball?"

This made Cassie laugh and she looked up with the hint of a smile on her face. "It definitely was not that," which made Max laugh too, his cheeks turning a bit red when their eyes met, but only momentarily, since Max couldn't hold the look for long.

"So what is it then?" he said to his own hands.

Cassie closed her eyes and could see a man made of shadows with the build of her father against the diffused light from her eyelids. "I don't know," she said quietly after opening her eyes. "It's weird…You wouldn't understand."

"Try me," Max said encouragingly.

Cassie took a deep breath to clear her mind. "Well, it's just…Well, I mean I was never really close to my father, you know? He was always away, always busy with his work and his research. And every time he was home and I tried to understand what he was doing, he would always tell me that I was too young, that I wouldn't understand. And then it was like the older I got, I kept waiting and hoping that one day I would somehow reach that point, you know? Like one day I would be old enough and I would understand. And then just when it felt like I was at that point, he was gone." Cassie stopped talking to look away and wipe a few tears that had come to her eyes. Max, always the gentleman, produced a napkin from his front pocket.

"Thanks," Cassie said, looking back at him with a smile, before wiping her eyes and blowing her nose.

"No problem," Max said while he began to blush furiously.

"So anyway," Cassie continued after collecting herself, "I came here to Israel because I wanted to be closer to him, to finally understand just what it was all about. And now that I'm actually really closer to my father than I've ever been before, I feel farther from him than I've ever been. Almost like all these things happening, all this weirdness, is pushing me to him and away from him at the same time. Does that make any sense?"

Max took a moment to look at Cassie, to really look at her. The only thing he wanted to do right then was to hug her and tell her that everything was going to be okay; that her father loved her dearly and even from beyond would not let anything bad happen to her, and that he and Frankie would always be there for her, no matter how bad these men who were haunting her smelled. But instead he just smiled, looked her in the eyes and said, "Not at all."

Cassie couldn't help but laugh. Then she punched him in the arm and said, "Thanks. I needed that."

"My pleasure," said Max. He opened his mouth as if he was about to say something else, but he stopped, and squinted his eyes, and instead of what he wanted to say, he said, "What now?"

Cassie turned to what Max was looking at and they both watched a small boy, probably five or six years old, with wispy black hair and a pale, round face, tiptoe his way along the fence. He did so slowly and carefully, as if walking a tightrope; as if no one could see him doing this in full daylight.

When the boy noticed Cassie and Max staring at him, he stopped, looked up and brought a finger to his mouth to say "Shush." Then he continued tiptoeing towards them.

Cassie turned around to exchange a weird look with Max.

Max offered the same look back and shrugged his shoulders. "If he's trying to be invisible it's not working," he whispered.

Cassie laughed and turned back around. The boy, who was now just a few feet away, was now leaned all the way over, practically crawling, making those last few feet take even longer to achieve.

Finally he made it to Cassie's side and straightened himself to his full height of three and a half feet. The boy frowned and looked quite distressed. "That was hard," he said.

Cassie shook her head and opened her mouth to say something but the boy shushed her again.

"Quiet, lady," he said in his high-pitched voice, lowering it to a whisper. "You are in much bad danger."

Cassie was still either too shocked or too amused to say anything. Luckily Frank, who had just approached with Kyle and Ryan in tow, was not. "Hey," he said loudly, "isn't that the kid at the hostel the other night with dad's journal?"

The boy looked up wide-eyed at Frank and shushed him too.

Cassie snorted with laughter. "I think," she said.

"Well, what does he want?" Frank asked Cassie while he playfully messed up the boy's hair. The boy swatted at Frank's hand with annoyance.

"He says we're in much bad danger," Max answered Frank.

Frank laughed and shook his head. "Way to state the obvious, kid," Kyle said from behind him.

"No kidding," Frank agreed, before he knelt down to eye level with the boy. "So who are you and what were you doing with our father's journal?"

The boy screwed up his eyes at Frank. "I, Key. I help. You must come. You must come now," he said.

"Key, huh?" Frank said amused. "What kind of name is that?"

"It my name," Key said confused, shaking his head.. "Come now and I tell. Please to come, yes?"

"Come where? What are you talking about?" Cassie finally chimed in.

Key took a deep breath as if he was trying to relax. "You no understand. Must leave. Very, very bad. I give book and you read and you understand, yes? But must go go go now! Please!"

Key looked very frustrated, which only further confused everyone around them, especially Cassie. "But our teacher," she tried to explain by speaking to the boy in his only broken English, "she in there, "Cassie pointed to the building behind them. "She talking to man. We go home. We leave this place."

Key's face dropped. "Oh no, lady. You no leave this place. You never leave this place. And teacher..." Key continued to sadly shake his head, "your teacher no more. Too late her, not too late you."

Frank shook his head and stood up. "God, is everybody crazy in this place? I am getting so sick of this! Can't people just talk normally and say what they're thinking? Why does everything have to be so freaking mysterious?"

Cassie glared at her brother. "Calm down, Frankie. He's just a kid.

And he did have dad's journal the last time we saw him."

"That's right!" Frank said wide-eyed, kneeling down again and grabbing Key by his little shoulders. "What were you doing with it? Did you steal it or something? If you don't take us to it, I swear to God I'm going to..."

Key cringed in fear as both Cassie and Max stood to stop Frankie from shaking him. "I will," Key was saying. "Please. I only help. Your father my father. Please," he kept saying.

Finally Frank let him go, allowing Key to cry into both his hands. "I'm sorry, kid," Frank said as he stood up, rubbing Key's head to try and make him feel better.

"I, Key. I help," Key said through his sobs. "Too late. Always too late."

Cassie, Frank and Max looked at each other in confusion. "I think we should go talk to Mrs. Ford about this," Cassie said.

"I think you're right," Frankie and Max agreed.

"Too late," Key continued to say through his sobs. "Go now. Must go now."

The urgency of his words from such a small child sent a chill down Cassie's spine, but she couldn't just leave Mrs. Ford. She remembered the way Mrs. Ford had said that they would all get through it together, and she believed her when she said it. She was not just going to leave her now.

Cassie turned to the entrance to the Embassy but Key blocked her way, pleading with her not to go. She knelt down in front of the boy. She gently to hold of him by the arms, and just as she was about to tell him not to worry, that everything was going to be all right, she heard it; one of the most terrible sounds she had ever heard, even worse than the sound of steel on stone. It was the sound of someone shrieking and it sounded like somebody she knew.

Cassie paused and lifted her head in order to hear it better, as did the rest of the group. It was like the sound a dying animal would make who was being suffocated, but different; more desperate, more hopeless. No words came out of it, just a long, slow shriek similar to the sound Mrs. Ford made the night before.

Cassie stood and turned in the direction of the building and the shriek. After what seemed like an eternity it finally ended, and the silence that followed it seemed almost as bad. But it did not last long. One single, definite, piercing gunshot shook the silence.

Cassie turned stunned to her brother Frank. "What's happening?" she demanded with both fear and uncertainty.

"I don't know," Frank said with a shake of his head.

Cassie's breathing was suddenly accelerated. The world was spinning. Everything was wrong. Nothing was right. She felt a tiny hand enter hers and she looked down into the large brown eyes of Key.

"We go now," he said simply. "We go fast now."

A window of the building opened and a man in sunglasses stuck his head out of it. He motioned to the guards standing outside who were on alert from the gunshot. The man held his hands out, apparently indicating that everything in the room was okay. Then the man motioned to the group. The guards looked at the man, confused. The man shook his head sternly and barked, "Get them."

The guards turned to the group. Max turned to Frank. Frank

turned to Cassie. Cassie turned to Key. Somebody said run. They did not hesitate; they ran, ran, ran like the wind.

CHAPTER 10 - THE PERFECT PB&J

Cassie wasn't sure at what point they lost the rest of the group. By the time she finally gained the courage to look behind her, she saw only Kyle and Ryan.

"No look. Just run," she heard Key say from in front of her, somehow aware of what she was doing although he never turned around.

She turned to Frankie and Max who ran at her side; neither shot her a glance. Both of them knew that if they saw the panic and the pain in her eyes they would not be able to continue.

Fleeing *who knew what*, continue they did. Jumping over a short wall they flew through a courtyard, then an archway, and finally curved around a fountain into a side door of an old synagogue. They surged through another door into a tiny alley, which ended at a large wooden door where they stopped; more accurately, where Key stopped and the rest followed suit.

They were all exhausted. Cassie leaned over, holding her knees, trying to regain her breath. Frankie and Max continued to nervously scan their surroundings. Kyle and Ryan collapsed to the ground by the wall.

"Why have we stopped?" Cassie asked Key, who was the only one who looked fine.

"Because we stopped," Key answered with a curious tilt of his head.

Cassie shook her own. "I know, but why?"

"Oh," Key said with a smile. Then he pointed at the large wooden door. "Behind the door to run no more," putting a hand on her shoulder. "You safe now, lady. But I check. You wait." Key sharply nodded his head once, not something Cassie would have expected from someone his age. Then he loped in the direction they came with his elbows out just like a Sunday jogger in Central Park.

Cassie shook her head and took a deep breath. When she closed her eyes she could see the shocked face of Mrs. Ford. She could hear the inhuman wail escaping from Mrs. Ford's open mouth. It echoed through her mind with no beginning or ending; just the sound, just the last sound a person would ever make.

"What have I done?" Cassie said to herself. She dropped to her knees and covered her face with her hands. "I killed her," she was saying through her tears, "It's my fault."

Frank put his hand on his sister's back. "It's not your fault," he said to her. "Maybe she's not dead. Maybe that wasn't her at all."

"Of course, she's dead!" Kyle angrily yelled from the wall. "Just like we're all going to be dead, much too soon!"

"Shut up, Kyle!" Frank yelled back. "Nobody's going to die! We'll be fine!"

"Dude," Kyle said, leaning forward with exasperation, "the

freaking American Embassy security just shot our teacher to death. We've got shadow men chasing us through the streets of Jerusalem. Even library books are trying to kill us. So please, for the love of God, tell me how we will possibly be fine."

"He's got a point there, Frank," Ryan added.

Frank looked back at both of them and just shook his head. He knew he had no answer for them, and, what's worse, he knew they were right. He might even have agreed with them, at least until Kyle mumbled loud enough to for him to hear, "It all your sister's fault anyway."

"That's it!" Frank said and his expression was like granite. He took his hand off of his sister's back and moving threateningly to Ryan and Kyle. They stood quickly to counter whatever Frank had in mind.

"Stop it!" Cassie yelled. "Just stop it now!"

None of the boys listened to her. Frank pushed Kyle in the chest. Kyle fell backwards but stopped himself from falling and came forward to push Frank back. Frank braced himself and didn't budge, so Ryan tried to come up behind Frank to hold him steady for Kyle. Meanwhile, Cassie continued to yell at them to stop it but to no avail. Finally she turned to Max and told him to do something.

Max had been watching with a stunned expression on his face. With everything happening, with everything that had happened, Max was slow to reconcile his thoughts with his feelings. He was still processing it when he met Cassie's eyes. He blinked his own twice, before slowly turning to the scuffle.

"Hey!" he yelled, the volume of his voice surprising even him.

They all stopped and turned to look at him.

"There is no such thing as a bad peanut butter and jelly sandwich!" he blurted out, saying the first thing that came to his mind.

Frank had Ryan in a headlock with Kyle on the ground with a hold of one of Frank's ankles, but they were all too stunned to continue the struggle. They just all stared at Max with curious looks on their faces.

Max, now with everybody's attention on him, was compelled to continue. "I mean think about it," he said. "Sometimes you don't have enough peanut butter but it's all good because then you just add extra jelly; makes the sandwich sweeter, yes, but you still get that occasional burst of peanut goodness." Max smiled widely. He was pacing now, speaking with his hands like a lawyer in court. "The same goes with not enough jelly and too much peanut butter. Or if you have too much of both, which is preferable if you think about it because inevitably it'll start oozing out and there's nothing quite like peanut butter and jelly ooze. But, and this is the most important part, let's say there's not enough of each. You think you're screwed, right? But you're not! You're not at all. Because even with just enough to get a taste, it's a reminder of that perfect peanut butter and jelly sandwich, that one where everything was just right, and that alone is enough to get you through that sandwich, with the promise of a future filled with perfect pb&j's. So you see when it's good it's good but even when it's not good it's fine because it can only get better. It can be even more perfect than the reality of just good or not good, cause reality is no match for... for..."

"For the dream that *is* the perfect peanut butter and jelly sandwich?" Ryan finished for him from the headlock.

"Exactly!" Max exclaimed, ending his pace to cross his arms authoritatively over his chest.

"And what does that have to do with this?" Frank asked confused.

"Everything," Max confidently said. "Or nothing," said with slightly less confidence. "But probably mostly nothing," Max concluded.

"Great," Kyle said from the ground, "now I really want a peanut butter and jelly sandwich."

"I do too," Cassie agreed wistfully.

"Same here," said Frank and Ryan at the same time.

They all paused to consider what it would be like to be eating the perfect peanut butter and jelly sandwich, regardless of whether it was perfect or not, since, as Max had just explained, it was impossible for a peanut butter and jelly sandwich to be imperfect.

Consequently, none of them noticed the large wooden door at the end of the alley open, or Key, whose head popped out of the opening. Somehow he had made it inside even though he had left in the opposite direction.

It was a strange sight to behold: Frank holding Ryan in a headlock with Kyle on the ground, both arms around one of Frank's ankles; Cassie bent over with her hands on her knees, her eyes unfocused, and her mouth open; Max standing above them all with his hands on his hips in a classic Superman pose. It would be a strange sight for most, but not for a boy like Key.

"Oh good!" he said. "We fight!" as he threw the door open and ran full speed at Frank, Ryan and Kyle. A rather majestic flying leap landed him on Ryan's back, straddling him as if he were a horse. A flurry of fists followed while Ryan yelled from the headlock, "Cut it out!"

Finally Cassie shook her head clear of perfect pb&js. "Key! What in God's name are you doing?" she said, standing up and taking a step towards him.

Key slowed the flurry to the pace of a Swedish massage. "*What?*" he asked innocently. "We fight, yes?"

"No!" Cassie said. Then she turned to Frank and commanded, "Let Ryan go already!"

Frank lifted his eyebrows with a shrug and released Ryan from the headlock. Ryan straightened up as Key slid off of his back. Key nearly landed on Kyle who still sprawled on the ground. Kyle stood and brushed himself off as much as possible.

Key looked at Cassie confused. "No fight?" he asked with a hint of disappointment.

"No, Key. No fight." she answered.

"Then what?"

Cassie turned around to look at Max as if she needed help explaining such a thing. Max responded with a shrug, which resulted in a very pointed stare from Cassie.

"Well, if you have to know," Cassie said to Key after turning back around, "we were idealizing peanut butter and jelly sandwiches to make us feel better about our impending deaths."

"Oh," Key said simply. "Smart, no," with a shake of his head, "American, yes," with a nod. He started walking towards the open door at the end of the alley. "All dead once," he said along the way. "And all dead again," he continued as they reached the door, where he stopped. "But not dead now," he concluded, motioning for them all to enter, which they did with Key bringing up the rear.

"Shoes off, please," was the last thing he said before he closed the door.

CHAPTER ELEVEN - SANCTUARY

The house was larger than expected from its modest sandstone exterior. The entryway opened into a large Tudor style hall paneled in dark mahogany. Floor to ceiling stained glass windows ran the length of it, depicting various scenes from Dante's Inferno. The hardwood floors were bathed in a myriad of colors. The space was at once depicting the chaos of the eternal descent and the serenity of a color splashed hallway.

The hallway, appropriately, ended in darkness. A woman dressed all in white emerged, walking slowly towards them while holding a fat black cat.

Cassie would have preferred to appreciate such a thing in silence, seeing a woman in white carrying a black cat walk slowly through all the colors of the Inferno, but she couldn't. At the same moment Ryan was arguing with Key over the removal of his shoes.

"But you don't understand," Ryan was saying, "I have a thing about my feet."

"But they your feet," was Key's response. "You love your feet. They *your* feet!"

Ryan could only shake his head, as he turned red, and continued to say, "You don't understand." But Key was intractable.

"Wait outside instead," he said with a shrug, which finally ended the argument, and Ryan reluctantly and finally removed his shoes just as the woman in white stopped in front of them.

"Ah, Ms. Lonely!" Key said, hurrying to her side to pet the top of the cat's head. It closed its golden eyes and smiled serenely.

"Ms. Lonely?" Frank said, after a curious glance at Cassie. "Is that the woman's, or the cat's name?" thinking he was making a joke.

Key frowned and said, "The cat's!" with a shake of his head. "This Abigail," referring to the woman in white, "but she no talk. Only cat. No her. Right, Abby?"

Abigail nodded followed by a meow from Ms. Lonely.

"See!" Key said with a smile, taking Abigail's hand in his own. "We go now. You follow."

Abigail nodded again, offering a flat smile to the group. Ms. Lonely just blinked. Then Abigail, Ms. Lonely, and Key turned and started walking down the long, colorful, Inferno hall. Cassie exchanged a look of disbelief with the others before following slowly behind the trio ahead of them down the hallway, through the darkness and into the library.

The library was twice the width of the hallway and just as long. The walls were lined with books, filling shelves some twenty feet high. Above them were spectacular works of art; classical, romantic, statuesque, and every adornment of the ages in between.

Ms. Lonely and Abigail waited at the entrance while the others wandered around the room in awe. Then Abigail quietly turned to go, exiting the room with a nod to Key's wave goodbye. No one else noticed that she was gone; they were all too busy being dumbstruck by the moment.

"This place is amazing, Key," said Cassie as she spun around on her heels taking it all in. What had impressed her most about Jerusalem since she arrived was how thousands of years of history, how the origins of so much she took for granted felt so alive. It was as if time moved like the tide; an eternal ebb and flow of the past and the present until it was all as real as the sound of the surf. The library was having the same effect on her, except the sound of the ocean in her ears was the silence of sanctuary yet still just as loud.

"Books old. Very old!" Key said. The others looked around in amazement. There were books against every wall, twenty feet high.

"Hey Key, do you think there are any books in here about the shadow men?" Frank asked, as he wandered around the room.

"Sure!" Key excitedly said. He motioned for Frank to follow him to a particularly ornate bookshelf. "Also my favorite," he told Frank as he removed a book and handed it to him.

Frank looked down at it confused, "The Giving Tree?"

Key nodded his head enthusiastically. "You read. I listen." He sat down on the floor and waited for Frank to do the same.

Frank didn't. "This is not what I mean, Key."

"Oh," Key said disappointed. He stood up and snatched the book from Frank's hands. "Constance answers. Constance knows and knows and knows."

Everyone looked curiously at each other. "Who's Constance?" Cassie asked, acting as the voice for the group.

Key didn't answer. He didn't have to. All he had to do was nod to the woman who was now standing in the entryway of the library.

"Welcome everyone," she said.

She was a tall, graceful woman; thin but definitely not frail. Her hair was cut short, and was pearl white. Her face was stern but pleasant and fair. Two men accompanied her, perhaps bodyguards, one man shutting the door after they entered. She didn't introduce them and they didn't speak.

"Please, please sit down," offered Constance.

Seven armchairs were arranged in a circle around a beautiful Persian rug in the center of the room. Constance took a seat in one of the armchairs and her men took their places obediently; one man to her right and one to her left. Cassie thought it a bit strange that Constance somehow knew the number of people who would suddenly show up at her house one day. Nonetheless, everyone sat, snugly settling into the chairs once they realized how long it had been since they had sat, let alone sat in such luxurious comfort.

"From what I gather," Constance began, speaking with the same grace with which she carried herself, "you have all had a pretty rough time of it. Unavoidable, I'm afraid, with circumstances being what they are." Constance crossed her arms at their wrists upon her lap, a maneuver that exuded calm and patience and something of gratitude. A sad smile played across her lips as she held Cassie's curious gaze. "Hello, Cassie. You have no idea how much it means to me to finally meet you."

Cassie narrowed her eyes but did not turn away from the eyes across from her. "What do you mean 'to finally meet me'? How do you even know who I am?"

"I knew your father. He was a dear friend and a colleague." She turned her attention to Frank who was sitting next to Cassie. "Hello, Frank." Then she turned to Max who was on the other side of Cassie, of course. "And you must be Max." Finally, completing the circle of eyes staring at her with, "And last but not least, Kyle and Ryan, yes?"

"Uh huh," Kyle and Ryan answered dumbly in unison.

"I, Key!" Key chirped.

Constance laughed, more with her eyes than with anything else. "Yes, Key, I know who you are."

Constance motioned to one of the men standing next to her. He quickly handed her a glass of brandy, which seemed to appear out of thin air. "Thank you, Brutus," she said to him from over her shoulder. Constance took a deep appreciative breath while she swirled the brandy around the glass. She took a sip. She smacked her lips. She said, "So what do you all think of our library?"

Max looked at Cassie. Cassie looked at Frank. Frank looked back at Cassie.

"It's awesome!" Kyle said while they were looking at each other.

Cassie could no longer contain herself. "*Awesome*? Awesome! Are you freaking kidding me?" Constance leaned back in her chair, looking calmer than ever. Cassie continued, leaning forward in her own. "We fly all the way out here to Israel, only to get chased through the streets at night by some scary weird shadow men. We meet up with the next weirdo wearing a top hat who tries to kill us with library books. When we make it to the embassy our teacher, our friend is killed. We finally wind up here at weirdo central and somehow you already know all of us and all our names and my father and all you ask... the most you can say... practically the first freaking thing out of your mouth... is, is, 'What do you think of the library?'!"

Cassie was leaning so far forward in her chair that if Max and Frank weren't holding onto her arms, she would have fallen face first onto the beautiful brown and gold weave Persian rug.

Constance's expression flattened. "Of course," she said, "my apologies." She took another long, slow sip of brandy. "So what would you like to know?"

Cassie's eyes went back to normal size. "Well, you could start with who you are!"

Constance nodded her head. "My name is Constance. I live here. I do my work here. I've known your father for many years, longer than even you've known him. He would not have mentioned me to you because, before this moment in time, there was no reason why you should know who I am. Now the time has come and you are here."

Cassie looked to the sky and back. "Okay, weird answer, but I guess I should have expected that."

"You did," Constance agreed. "You just didn't know you did."

Cassie sighed and shook her head. "Weirder still but whatever," she mumbled. "And how exactly do you know who I am without ever seeing me before, or all of us for that matter?"

Constance tilted her head. "I know because you know."

Cassie was shaking her head so much she was afraid it might fall off. Frank spoke up for her.

"Why do you have to talk like that? I mean seriously! Can't you just answer a freaking question?"

"My dear Frank," Constance said trying to hide her amusement, "just because you do not understand the answer does not make it any less an answer."

It was Frank's turn to shake his head now, and he did so with his mouth still open. Finally he turned to Cassie, who let out a deep breath she had been holding in an effort to calm herself.

"Okay," she said, "I get this whole mysterious we-know-everything-and-you-don't thing you have going on, but please, *please*, just answer one question for us, and pretend you're a normal person when you answer, okay?"

This time Constance didn't try to hide her amusement. "I will try my best," she said with a nod of her head.

"Good!" Cassie said with a nod of her own. "Please, like a normal, regular person, tell us why we are here."

"Are you sure that is the question you want to ask?" Constance asked with her glass of brandy closing on her lips.

"Positive!" Cassie said positively.

Constance sipped her brandy, letting the liquid slosh around her mouth before swallowing it. "Well," she began, "if you must know, you, Cassie, are here to save the world, or at least all the people living in the world, otherwise known as humankind, and though we are not sure exactly how you will accomplish this, we *are* sure that only you can. Do you feel better now?"

"Much," Cassie said confidently, as the answer slowly made its way to her brain. "Wait... I mean... *huh?*"

Constance laughed this time out loud, something she must not have been used to doing because it literally came out as a "Ha!" Then she handed her empty glass to the man named Brutus and said, "I think it would be best if we all eat now and get a good night's sleep. Who's hungry?"

"I am!" squeaked Key.

"Shut up, Key," Cassie blurted out, quickly realizing her rudeness and apologizing to Key. "I mean," she said to Constance, "did you just say that I was going to save the world?"

"Yes," Constance said, already standing, "Now what would everyone like to eat?"

Perhaps it was the shock of the moment, but everyone simultaneously answered, "Peanut butter and jelly," except, of course, for Ryan, who said, "Taco Bell."

CHAPTER TWELVE - GUARDIANS OF THE GARDEN

The dining room was much smaller than one would expect from a house so large. The space was long and narrow, and the table, which stretched the entire length of the dining room, was thin but cozy. A fire blazed in the fireplace in the far wall and above the mantle hung a majestic portrait of a man over six feet tall, with deep blue eyes, sharp cheeks and full lips that tipped down just at the edges. His hair was long, thick, and the color of winter raspberries. He was wearing a black robe and behind him, the sun set over a hill marked by large wooden crosses with blurred figures upon them. His expression and the way the light radiated from the horizon made the painting seem like a photograph of a man posing in front of the crucifixion of Jesus.

The portrait went unnoticed by all of them except Cassie, who continued to stare at it even after she sat down. There was something familiar about the man and she thought that if she stared at it long enough, she would be able to see her reflection in his deep blue eyes. But then the food appeared, and though she had no appetite at the moment, it was more appealing to stare at than the painting of the man.

Brutus and the other man carefully laid the food upon the table. The feast included a large platter of peanut butter and jelly sandwiches, plates of tabouli, hummus, pita and roast chicken. Everyone also was poured a glass of chai tea with cinnamon and cream. The aroma was intoxicating.

Constance sat at the end of the table closest to the fireplace. "Thank you, Brutus and Tiberius," she said to the two men after they had placed all the food upon the table. "That will be all."

Brutus looked at Tiberius. Tiberius looked at Brutus and they both looked at Cassie who narrowed her eyes at them when she realized she was the object of their attention. Both men turned back to Constance. "Are you sure?" Brutus asked.

Constance looked as if she wanted to rise to her feet in anger, but she quickly calmed herself and pursed her lips. "Yes, quite," she said.

Brutus looked back at Tiberius, who looked back with a shrug. Then both men exited the dining room through a side door that led to the kitchen.

"So," Constance said with a smile to all of them, "shall we eat?"

"We freaking shall!" Max said, excitedly grabbing a peanut butter and jelly sandwich.

They all began filling their plates with food. Key, who had never had a peanut butter and jelly sandwich before, ate five in succession.

"Don't think Americans are so stupid now, do you, Key?" Frank said while eating one of his own.

"No," Key answered with his mouth full. "Still stupid. But good sandwich!"

Frank shook his head then noticed his sister was just staring at the food. He elbowed her and said, "What's wrong? Why aren't you eating?"

"Oh, I don't know," she answered without looking at him. "I guess being told that you're supposed to save the world can have an effect on your appetite."

Frank shook his head. "Yeah, but she's a weirdo," Frank spoke before realizing the weirdo in question was sitting three seats away and well within earshot. He turned to her with a hand up and a "No offense." Constance smiled graciously as to say "None taken" Frank turned back to Cassie. "Don't take her seriously or anything. Obviously if anybody is going to save the world, it'd be me."

"Oh, really?" Cassie answered with a snort. "And why is that obvious?"

Frank stuffed some roast chicken in his mouth. "What do you mean?" he said indignantly. "I have all of the classic good looks of a superhero. Plus everyone knows I got all the brains in the family. Not to mention my strength, my tenacity, my resolve, and, and I know no fear." He concluded his explanation with a smirk and a spoonful of tabouli, which he nearly choked on.

"*No fear*?" Cassie replied with a smirk of her own. "What about sock puppets?"

"Okay," Frank admitted, "sock puppets freak me out. But that's only because of that dream I had when my feet *actually* turned into sock puppets and tried to eat me."

"What about people with braces?" Max added.

Frank nodded his head. "Okay, them too, but that's because of Poltergeist Two."

"And clown dolls?" Cassie added.

"Poltergeist One," Frank answered with a more emphatic nod of his head.

"And mirrors," Max threw in.

"Again, part one. But," Frank tried in his defense, "ironically enough, I'm not afraid of poltergeists at all."

A smattering of laughter made its way around the table, ending with Ryan turning red and standing, pointing up at the ceiling. "Look up in the air! It's a bird... It's a plane..."

"Eh, it's just Stupidman," Kyle finished for him.

Another round of laughter, this time with more enthusiasm, except, of course, for Frank who rebutted with "Oh yeah, well you're... you're... you're Superstupidman!" Cassie was still lost in thought at the idea of actually being the one appointed to save the world.

As the laughter died down, the boys returned to the feeding and distracting themselves from reality with trivialities. These included, among other things, the various super powers of Stupidman. Apparently his main superpower was to be so dumb the bad guys would kill themselves rather than have to listen to him.

Regular non-superheroes could use the Stupidgun. When a person was hit with its projectiles it would make them say things like "Not to ask a stupid question but..." before they would ask a stupid question, or "I just read the most interesting article on the internet..." and by 'article' mean blog.

Last but not least was the Stupidmobile, which was just a typical city bus filled with all the typical people one would find on a typical city bus and which would still make all the stops even when Stupidman was on his way to stop a bank robbery, or rushing to his mom's house to unclog her toilet.

Cassie for her part could not distract herself from reality, no matter how much she tried to. When she was not pushing her food around on her plate, she was staring at the unreadable, expressionless face of Constance. When she was not doing that, she was staring at the portrait above the fireplace. There was something in the man's eyes that almost brought Cassie knowledge of something she didn't know she knew.

"Perhaps God wants me to see something in his eyes," she mumbled to herself.

"Perhaps," she thought she heard mumbled from the end of the table, perhaps from Constance, perhaps from the man in the portrait.

Cassie shook her head. Tears came to her eyes and when she wiped them away with her hand was when she saw it. From the corner of her eye, in the doorway in darkness, the shadow of a man, but too tall to be just a man, arms too long and too thin to just be arms, the same man, the same shadow, the same thing over and over again.

There was no fear this time. Her heart did not skip a beat. Her breath was not lost from her lungs. This was not fear she was feeling. This was anger. And her jaw clenched. And she made fists with her hands. And her whole body felt like it had turned to steel. She had never felt such anger before, but she had had enough. Enough of shadow men, enough of the unknown, enough of being led through life by the hand of someone she didn't know. Cassie had had enough of fart jokes, enough answers that weren't answers, enough death and dying and smelling, and enough of watching the people she loved leave her all alone. She had had enough of everything.

"Enough!" she yelled, slamming her fists upon the table and standing up to turn to the doorway. But there was nothing. Just shadows dancing in the firelight.

She would have expected to feel relieved. She would have expected a sudden calmness. But there wasn't.

"Damn it all to hell!" she cried, sitting back down hard in her chair and looking up to see everyone staring at her.

All of them looked stunned, except for Constance, of course, who looked as if she expected such a thing. She didn't even stop chewing on the chicken she was eating.

"And don't give me that look!" Cassie shot at her.

Constance swallowed, slowly. "What look, dear?" she asked amused.

"And don't call me dear!" Cassie shook her head and took a deep breath. She didn't care that everybody was staring at her with their mouths opened. She didn't care that she was biting down so hard that the muscles of her jaw were twitching. She didn't care that everyone in Israel seemed to be after her, even the shadows. She didn't care about anything anymore.

Constance opened her mouth to say something else, either that or to take another bite of her chicken.

"Don't!" Cassie stopped her. "I am so sick and tired of being treated like a child! Save the world? Save the freaking world? Well, what if I don't want to! You're going to give me some answers and you're going to give them to me now!"

Constance lips creased into a flat smile. She delicately wiped the corners of her mouth with the tip of her napkin. She turned to Cassie with a look of complete and utter satisfaction. "But," she began.

"Be quiet!" Cassie stopped her again. "Who are the shadow men?" she demanded.

"They are the servants of the Guardians," Constance answered without hesitation.

"And who are the Guardians?" Cassie continued to demand.

"They protect the Garden," was the answer.

"And what is the Garden?"

"The Garden is what the Guardians call the Earth."

"And what do the shadow men do?"

"They take peoples' souls, at least from the ones who still have them."

Cassie's jaw flinched again. "So let me get this straight...The Guardians are trying to protect the Earth by sending out these *shadow men* to take everybody's souls, yes?"

"Yes," Constance answered with a nod of her head.

Cassie shook her own. She was still not satisfied. "Why?"

Constance put her napkin down beside her plate. She swallowed hard. She seemed as if she was trying to formulate an answer.

"Why?" Cassie yelled, slamming her fist on the table again.

Constance looked up with something like eternity shining within her eyes. "We don't know," she answered simply.

"They don't know," Cassie mumbled to herself while looking down at her untouched plate of food. "So, in conclusion," she said looking back up at Constance, "these *Guardians of the Garden* have sent out these *shadow men* to suck out our souls, but we don't know why, and it's my job to stop them, but we don't know how, yes?"

"Yes," Constance said with a final nod of her head.

"Gee! Why was that so hard?" Cassie crossed her arms over her chest and sighed. "All you had to do was say that from the start. *Hello. My name is Constance and you are going to save the world from soul-sucking shadow men*. Perhaps then I'd be able to eat."

"Cassie? I do apologize for the misunderstanding. I tend to softly reveal difficult truth and this time, I failed to see through your eyes. Let's just eat and discuss other matters after we have broken bread," apologized Constance. Cassie, who had been sitting with crossed arms, uncrossed them, grabbed a drumstick from her plate and voraciously tore into it. "Can someone pass the salt?" she asked with her mouth full.

Everybody was too stunned to respond. They were still staring at her with their mouths opened. It was Constance, of course, who passed a saltshaker to Max to pass it to Cassie. Max held it in the air in front of him for a second as if he didn't know what it was. Constance had to tap him on the shoulder to reanimate him.

Finally the salt was passed, Max's eyes filled with awe as he handed it to her. Cassie sprinkled salt all over her plate, too ravenous to even say thank you to Max.

Max laughed to himself, then lifted his glass of Chai and said, "Here's to Cassie Lint the shadow slayer, and soon to be savior of the world."

Everyone laughed too and raised their glasses. Cassie only mumbled "Yeah, yeah" as she continued to eat.

CHAPTER THIRTEEN - EVEN ANGELS HAVE SHADOWS

The bedroom was modest considering the size of the manor: two twin beds, a couple of nightstands and a large armoire. Two white curtained windows looked out onto the courtyard in the center of the manor, or what was assumed as the center since the maze of stairways and hallways leading in every which direction made it hard to know where they were. A portrait hung on the wall between the beds.

It was of Constance sitting in the library. Directly behind her stood Brutus and Tiberius, their arms at their sides Secret Service style. To the left of Brutus and Tiberius were Abigail and Ms. Lonely, and to their right was Key. A fire blazed in the fireplace behind them all, lending an edge of darkness to all their faces and casting long shadows from their feet all except for Constance. Constance looked younger and brighter, as if she absorbed the light rather than reflected it. Constance was also the only one looking straight ahead; everyone else looked away, either at the floor, the walls, or at one another.

"Maybe what she sees is more important than what we see," Cassie said to herself when she first saw the painting. But now it was three o'clock in the morning and she was lying in bed and she was still thinking about it.

Her brother was asleep in the bed next to hers, snoring away. The others were located somewhere else in this maze of a manor.

Dinner ended in peanut butter and jelly delirium caused the combination of stress, no sleep and too much sugar. Kyle and Ryan were making lists of who should and should not be saved by Cassie. Atop the list of 'who shouldn't' was Michael Bay for the sin of screwing up *Transformers 2*. As for 'who should', it ran the gamut from Will Ferrell to Batman to Charles Barkley to Harry Potter. It did not seem to matter whether their entries were real or not. The only thing that did seem to matter was that they were not family members or friends or anybody that either one personally knew.

Frank and Max tried not to participate in deference to Cassie, who spent the rest of the meal in contemplative, silent consumption. However, sometimes it was just too tempting, especially when it came to the suckiness of Michael Bay.

The discussion and dinner finally came to an end when Key leaned face forward into his tabouli, too tired to hold his head up any longer.

Constance led them up the stairs to their rooms. She did so in the dark with but a candelabrum for light. When asked why she didn't just turn on the lights, she answered, "Because darkness is easier to see with candlelight," which resulted in a bout of low grumbling and head shaking from the group.

Finally they arrived where Cassie was now. Frank insisted on sleeping in the same room. "For her protection," he said, but Cassie knew better. As kids, whenever they saw a scary movie he would sneak into her room at night and sleep on the floor, and given the fact that they were now being hunted by shadow men and that they had just talked about *Poltergeist One* and *Two*, she was not surprised by his choice of rooms.

She only noticed the painting in passing as she made her way to the bed. She thought that once she lied down she would sleep, but there was no sleep. So she got up to look at the picture. In the darkness, it seemed to illuminate itself, and the longer she looked into the painted eyes looking back at her, the more it felt like she was looking at her father.

She wiped the tears from her eyes and threw herself back into bed, wondering what it was about the eyes that could cause such a reaction in her. The shadow men did not have eyes to speak of, just black spots in indented sockets, reminding her of her father those nights before he would leave for another trip. His flights always seemed to leave late, after her bedtime, but there would be no sleep either those nights. Cassie would lie in bed waiting for her father to open her door. It seemed to take forever, but finally she would hear his heavy footsteps on the wooden floors, and he'd open her door, and he'd stand there in the doorway with the light behind him, casting his entire body in shadow. Cassie hated these nights because she never knew how long it would be before she would see her father again. So even though she waited all night for him to open her door, when he would open her door she would shut her eyes. She would just lie there and listen to the way he breathed, heavy and labored, punctuated by sadness. And it wasn't until right before he would close her door that she would crack open her eyes and search out in the darkness for his own. But she could never find them. All she could ever see were two black spots where she knew they were. And she always wondered if he was looking back at her too, or if he had already looked away.

So now it was three in the morning and there were still tears in her eyes and she couldn't dismiss the memory no matter how hard she tried. Frankie continued to snore. Nobody was standing at the door. Somewhere, someplace, men made of shadows were lurking, waiting to suck out the soul of the world. And somewhere else, someone else was waiting for Cassie to save it.

"How can I save the world if I can't even fall asleep?" she mumbled as she got out of bed for the second time that night.

She walked to the window and looked out at the courtyard in the center of the manor. It was something out of a childhood fantasy complete with fountain, reflecting pool and marble statues of cherubs and angels. The moon was full, spilling light across the Poplars and into the water. It was a reminder that beautiful things still existed in the world, no matter how much ugliness people were capable of doing to ruin it.

"Maybe it's just a matter of what we choose to look at," she said to herself.

"Maybe it's a matter of what chooses to look at us," as she stared at one of the angels in the courtyard, waiting for it to stare back at her. It didn't.

"Whatever," she said with a shrug. "Even angels have shadows."

She got back into bed and pulled the covers tight. As she listened to her heartbeat another sound interrupted the flow, a scuttling sound.

It came from Frankie's side of the room and last time she checked, Frankie didn't scuttle.

Cassie sat up and gazed into the shadows. Once again the world was playing tricks on her, and she held her breath and stared into the darkness.

And there it was. Sitting at the edge of the massive armoire was a spider at least as large as a medium-sized dog.

Her first thought was to scream but what if the thing had sensitive hearing. What would she do then? It would probably get testy and want to bite, or whatever dog-sized spiders scuttling out of supersized dressers do when they're alarmed by screaming teenage girls. To make matters worse, it was quite hairy.

"Don't panic," Cassie thought immediately realizing that that would be precisely the thing to do at such a moment.

She picked up the alarm clock from the nightstand next to the bed and threw it across the room, hitting her brother in the shoulder.

Frankie sat up in bed, looking dazed and rubbing his shoulder. "What the freak?" he said with a weary look of death at Cassie.

"Be quiet," she whispered, pointing in the direction of the spider.

"I was asleep. How much more quiet could I have been, you dork!"

Cassie shushed him again and pointed more emphatically at the armoire.

Frankie sighed, knowing that he had to turn around to see what she was pointing at, but at the same time, not wanting to turn around at all. This was the scene in *Poltergeist One* when you turn to look at what's behind you and a possessed clown doll is staring back at you.

"I don't want to know," he said simply.

"You will once you do," Cassie answered. Realizing how what she just said sounded like something Constance would say, she shook her head and mumbled to herself, "It's freaking contagious or something."

Frankie's eyes opened wide. "Oh, jeez! Is something on me? Cassie, you have to tell me now." Frankie whipped off his shirt and threw it to the floor. "Is it gone?"

She pointed again. This time he turned around. He squinted in the dark until it registered.

The spider beast scuttled again, turning in a circle before heading straight for Frankie's bed.

"Holy crap!" he said as he leaped out of his bed and into hers.

She was impressed. She had never seen her brother move so fast. "Wow, Frank!"

"Shut up, Cass! What the hell is that?"

The spider leaped upon Frankie's bed and started to make spiderlike movements to give itself more comfort. Like a dog, it turned in circles a few times, dug up the bedding a little, and then rested.

"Oh my God," mouthed Cassie.

"Yeah!" said Frank.

"Should we turn on a light?" she asked.

"I think we should run for it," replied Frankie, his eyes wide with horror. "That thing's as big as grandpa's poodle."

"Grandpa's poodle was a biter."

"No kidding!"

Just as Cassie and Frank were about to run for it the door to the bedroom opened. It was Constance. She flipped on the light. "I see you've met Willie." She walked the length of the room and sat down on the bed next to the spider. "I hope she didn't scare you too badly. She's quite harmless," she said, petting Willie's tummy. "You've been a naughty girl, haven't you?" Constance continued to pet the thing. After a few seconds of reassurance she looked up at the twins. They were still in shock.

"She wouldn't harm a fly," said Constance, looking down at Willie, who was quivering with delight from all the loving attention she was getting. "She loves getting her belly scratched. Don't you, muffin?" Willie started to wiggle once again.

"She's harmless?" stuttered Frank.

"I wouldn't say harmless. She is extremely lethal when she wants to be. After all, she weighs nearly fifteen pounds and her bite is quite deadly." Constance picked up Willie to expose her fangs. "These little teeth are over six inches long. If the venom doesn't kill you the bite most definitely will."

"Six inches," said the twins in unison.

"Would either of you want to hold her. She loves to make new friends."

"No!!!" They cried in unison once again.

"Oh, you guys are going to hurt Willie's feelings. Not all things are what they seem. We have teeth too. That doesn't mean we go around biting people. Besides, Willie's job is to help protect the household. And she knows you two are a part of this household."

114

Willie stood upright when she heard her name, like a dog standing on its hind legs.

The twins looked at each other in disbelief. Frankie shrugged his shoulders. Cassie mouthed the word 'Whatever'.

"I'll give it a go," said Frankie finally.

Cassie moved away from her brother, keeping a safe distance from what was about to happen.

"All you have to do," stated Constance, "is call her name and tell her to come. I promise you she's harmless."

Frankie looked at Cassie and then to Constance. He then looked across at Willie, who seemed eager to pounce.

"Frankie, you'll be fine. Just call her name."

"Here, Willie," offered Frank, with a whisper.

Willie jolted to attention, standing upright on all eight legs. She looked excited, or deadly; Frankie couldn't tell which, but continued to hold out his arms as if to catch a large beach ball or a giant, mutant, poisonous, hairy spider.

Willie danced in circles a couple of times with excitement and then leapt into Frankie's arms. At first Frankie was terrified; Willie's legs were a bit sticky and covered with small barbs. It didn't hurt, but it was a tad disquieting.

"Be good for mother, Willie and don't overdo it." Willie reacted to Constance's voice by snuggling down into Frankie's arms. She seemed contented, but not as much as Frankie who could not contain the smile on his face.

Cassie had never seen him so happy. "*Really*?" she said.

Willie turned over in Frankie's arms, offering him her underbelly.

Frankie scratched her abdomen and her arms legs flailed excitedly. "Check it out, sis. She's ticklish!"

Cassie smiled a nervous smile, backing away. "That's great, Frank."

Constance stood up. She looked pleased at how well the two were getting along. "Frankie, sweetheart," she said, "be a doll and take care of Willie tonight. I need to borrow your sister. My husband would like to meet her."

The twins looked puzzled. Constance had never mentioned a husband before.

"Your husband?" Cassie asked surprised.

"Now?" Frankie asked at the same time.

"Yes, my husband," Constance answered. "Yes Frankie, now."

CHAPTER FOURTEEN - LUCY, I'M HOME

Like everything else that had been happening to her lately, the walk down the stairs to meet Constance's husband felt unreal and dreamlike. Candle light flickered, shadows danced, and the eyes of every portrait hanging along the stairwell seemed to follow their every step.

Down the hallway, they strode and then made a right leading to another hallway. This hallway was twice the length of the first and contained no doors or windows. Many turns later Constance and Cassie stood before and then entered through a modest wooden door. Entrance through the door led onto the landing of a staircase that circled the walls like the descending pirouette of a lovely ballerina.

The first thing Cassie did was look over the banister. It seemed to go as far up as it did down, and since neither ceiling nor floor could be seen in the darkness, the length in either direction appeared impossibly endless.

"How far down does it go?" Cassie whispered to Constance.

"All the way to the bottom," Constance answered, causing a sigh from Cassie as she realized that she should have expected such an answer.

It was at that point, Cassie decided not to say another word. It seemed every answer from Constance was just Cassie's question phrased in a different way. It was while walking behind Constance down what seemed to be an endless, circular staircase Cassie noticed how quiet Constance was. Cassie admired the graceful way Constance carried herself, but being with her, was almost like being alone; the stairs didn't even creak from the weight of her steps.

"How odd," Cassie thought, but not as odd as the paintings on the wall, which quickly drew Cassie's attention. They were all portraits of men and they all had the same amused expression. It was as if someone had just whispered something funny into their ears. The only change from one portrait to another was the degree of amusement. Some portrait faces were grinning, others were smiling, and a few seemed about to laugh. Cassie kept expecting the next portrayed face to have reverted to the painter's originally painted expression. However, after the first ten portraits, then twenty, then thirty, she learned what not to expect.

"How strange," Cassie thought, but not as strange as the effect the candlelight had on the far wall of the stairwell. The banister was made of oak and carved throughout the posts and rail was a complicated sequence of vines. They were curving into and out of each other, sometimes intertwined into something of a fist before branching out again. Sometimes the branches spread about to allow room for flowers to blossom, sometimes not seeming like something that had been carved at all. It was if the entire structure had grown from the ground up.

"It's all so beautiful," thought Cassie. However, her attention was caught by the shadows the carved bannister created on the far wall. The vines appeared as bodies, the flowers as wings. When the candlelight fluttered, the bodies and flower wings became one, so that to Cassie it seemed like they were being accompanied by an audience of angels as they made their way down the stairs. Flickering candlelight wavered like fluttering wings as if all of heaven's angels applauded their every step.

"How weird," she thought, but not as strange at how quiet Constance was; almost as if she wasn't even there. Cassie thought it strange because there were so many things they could be talking about. Cassie had just been told that she was supposed to save the world. She had just been told that her father was a close friend of Constance. She had just met a giant, hairy spider named Willie. Any of these things seemed reasonable topics of conversation, and yet Constance continued to take each deliberate step down the stairs in silence. And with all these unknowns swirling around unanswered within her head, it was understandable that one question would evolve from the rest; the question of 'Why me?'

Constance cleared her throat, causing the candlelight to quiver and the shadows of angels' wings to clap. "What you have failed to consider, my dear Cassie," Constance said without turning around, "is that your silence is as meaningful as mine."

Cassie stared at the back of Constance's head, knowing somehow that Constance could see her doing this. Cassie wanted to ask how Constance knew what Cassie was thinking, but a question like that didn't seem worth asking anymore. So instead she asked, "What do you mean that my silence is as meaningful as yours?"

"It means," Constance stated, "that sometimes the act of asking the question is more important than the question itself. *Asking* the question can prove to be just as cathartic as receiving the answer you'd like to hear."

"Okay then," Cassie said defiantly. "Why am I supposed to be the one to save humanity; save the world?"

Constance paused before she answered, and by the quivering candlelight, Cassie could tell Constance was laughing to herself. "See?" Constance smilingly said. "Now doesn't that feel better Cassie?"

"Not really," Cassie mumbled as the bottom of the stairway came into view.

Cassie's first sight was of modest hardwood floors, and then, as the reach of the candlelight expanded, she marveled at the two massive gold doors set deep into the manor's wall.

Gracefully pivoting to face Cassie, Constance announced, "And just as quickly as the journey began, it seems we have arrived," Constance had stopped before the massive doors. Cassie stopped as well. "Yeah, if arriving after an eternity can be said to be quick."

"You have no idea how long eternity is, my dear," Constance answered, her smile widening. "And let's hope you never will."

"Amen to that," Cassie said with a nod, leaning back on her heels as if anxious to take the next step in her journey to meet Constance's husband.

Constance's smile faded as her eyebrows rose and presented an elegant curve above her eyes. "Are you ready?" she asked with her hand on the door handle.

Cassie set both feet firmly on the ground and responded somewhat sarcastically, "This conscript is ready for more, Ma'am!" She stood saluting with, hopefully, a stony expression on her face.

Constance tilted her head as though Cassie's brave response had impressed her. Then Constance opened the left hand gold door that looked to weigh a thousand pounds with just a small turn of the knob and a light push.

Behind the massive door was the smallest room of the manor she had seen. It was even smaller than her bedroom at home. The walls were lined with books; a mini-library. However, the bookshelves were uneven. It was as if they had been carved from the very manor walls by someone with nervous hands. The ceiling and floor were made of smooth stone; the fireplace carved from the stone wall was obviously the work of the 'someone' with nervous hands. The fireplace's dancing flames as the only source of light within the room. Above the mantle was another portrait. This one was of Constance. She had a Mona Lisa smile and behind her was a tree bearing bright red fruit. In front of the fireplace sat two large armchairs seemingly carved out of the same material as the banister of the stairs and by the same artist. The backs of the chairs resembled the back of some mythical creature and the armrests ended in clawed, bony hands grasping something like crossed stakes that also acted as chair legs. Antlers rose from the top of the armchairs in front of the fireplace casting curious shadows upon the smooth stone floor; the shadow of an angel, the shadow of a devil, and sometimes a shadow figure that resembled her father. Cassie stared to find another look at her father's shadow.

It is not polite to stare," Cassie heard. She turned toward the softly commanding voice.

It was a man's voice, deep and powerful and yet soft at the same time. It would have startled her, because it seemed as if one of the chairs had said it, but there was something familiar about the situation; something comforting.

"Um... sorry?" she said, not sure why she was apologizing for staring at shadows.

"Your apology is accepted," the voice came back with a throaty chuckle. Smoke rose from one of the chairs, forming a nearly perfect ball but for a smoke trail from the source of where it was exhaled. It reminded her of the two-dimensional sperm in her High School Health videos. But then its creator rose and all other subjects fled from her mind.

He was tall, maybe six foot three or four. He had deep blue eyes and full comfortable lips that tipped down just at the edges. His hair was long and thick, the color of winter raspberries.

He was smoking a cigar, which he casually extinguished in the ashtray on the coffee table, stooping slightly to do so, then rising again to his full impressive height and turning to Cassie.

A feeling of déjà vu overwhelmed her. It was more than just his voice that struck her as familiar. The fire, the shadows, the look in his eyes seemed too unreal to be real, or perhaps too real. Cassie stood with her mouth slightly open, trying to follow the thread of memory back to its source; trying to unravel the mystery of the moment. Was it because she had stared at his portrait for so long that his image and the look in his eyes were imprinted on her brain? Had this all happened before in a dream? Cassie wondered how long she would stand there in silence before she would know for sure.

"You don't seem surprised to see me," she heard, waking her from her reverie.

Cassie blinked her eyes and looked back at him, surprised. That was precisely how she thought she looked. "I'm sorry," she began.

"You already said that," he said with a further curl of his lips.

Cassie shook her head. "I know… it's been a long night." She took a step towards him and held out her hand. "I'm…"

"Cassandra," he said, interrupting her. "I am well aware of who you are." His hand felt surprisingly cold in hers. He did not shake her hand instead he placed his hand flat in her own and covered the back of her hand with his large, manicured thumb. He released her hand and motioned to the open chair.

"Nobody ever calls me Cassandra," she said, somewhat dazed as she proceeded to sit down.

The man sat down as well. "Well, then I'll be the first."

"Okay, whatever," Cassie mumbled while rubbing her hands in her lap in an effort to warm them once again. She looked back at him and said, "I'm sorry," for a third time. "Stop saying you are sorry!" Cassie quickly thought. Trying to salvage whatever small conversation they had been having, Cassie told him, "I still don't know your name."

"You don't?" the man said with something of a smile. "Then I'm the one who should be apologizing." The man massaged his thick lips around his teeth as if he was deciding what his name was. "You can call me Lucy," he finally decided.

"*Lucy?*" The absurdity of such a large man being named Lucy, allowed Cassie to relax, and she smiled as she leaned back to continue, "Do you mean like Lucy on the *I Love Lucy* television show*?* Even I know that show and you're *a lot* older than I am!"

Lucy crossed one leg over the other and rested his hands on it. "Age is relative, my dear Cassandra," he answered. "And I'm afraid I despise television." Lucy scoffed at the word with a wave of his hand. "The illusion of offering hope in half hour segments is nearly an abomination. If only the hope*less* bought as much laundry detergent and toothpaste as the hope*ful*. At that point there might be something decent to watch. Otherwise, it's all the same drivel."

Cassie had to stifle a laugh. She appreciated this kind of weirdness much more than Constance's version of it. "Even Seinfeld?" she asked with a smile on her face.

By the look on Lucy's face, he was enjoying himself as well. "Don't get me started on Seinfeld! Constance was addicted to it."

This time Cassie did allow herself to laugh. "So was my mom," she said. "And where did Constance go anyway? She was right behind me the whole time."

The smile on Lucy's face spread, revealing a rather large set of teeth. "You'll get used to it. I certainly have. One minute she's there, the next...*poof!*"

"No kidding!" Cassie said with a snort. "It seems as though even when she's with me, it feels like she's not."

Lucy nodded his head in agreement, never taking his eyes off of Cassie's.

Cassie took a deep breath through her nose. She was finally starting to feel better about things, though she couldn't really define why. The way Lucy looked at her reminded her of how she should look at herself in the mirror on all of those mornings when she was trying to decide just who she was. It was a curious thought, but she liked it.

"So is Lucy short for something?" she asked.

"It is," Lucy said with a nod of his head.

Cassie waited for an answer but none was forthcoming. "Are you going to tell me your full name?"

"Guess," Lucy smirked.

"Hmm," Cassie stalled. "Is it something European like Lucander or something strange like that?"

"No," Lucy laughed. "It's not Lucander but you're close."

"Is it Luke?"

"Nope."

"Something crazy like Alouicious, huh?"

"No, it's not, but that's a good one."

Cassie leaned forward and inspected him as if his name was written on his forehead. "It's Lucille, isn't it? You were just too embarrassed to tell me!"

Lucy seemed to be thoroughly enjoying this game and he laughed heartily. "No, it is certainly not Lucille."

Cassie paused again, waiting for him to give her the answer. Lucy just smiled mischievously back at her. "You're not going to tell me, are you?"

Lucy lifted his eyebrows. "No, I'm not."

"Whatever," Cassie said. "I'll figure it out!" She leaned back heavily in her chair and crossed her arms defiantly over her chest. Somehow the stranger things became the more normal they seemed. Cassie was just starting to get used to it. "So why did you want to see me anyway? You heard I was going to save the world and you wanted my autograph or something? Or are you finally going to tell me what is going on around here?"

Lucy took a deep breath, flaring his nostrils as he did. "I simply wanted to meet you. We've all heard..."

"Yeah, yeah," Cassie interrupted him. "This is the Matrix and I am 'the one' and you have all been *awaiting* my arrival."

Cassie looked around at the room that had been carved out of stone: the strange armchairs, the books bound in blood red leather, the fireplace which continued to blaze though no wood was to be found and realized how appropriate it was for the room to be such a reflection of Lucy.

She shrugged her shoulders and returned her attention to Lucy, who looked back at her while holding in his silent laughter concerning Cassie's words and attitude.

"Do you mind if I smoke?" he asked, already leaning forward to retrieve his cigar.

"No," Cassie responded with another shrug. "Whatever. This is your house. Smoke some weed for all I care."

"Constance said I should watch my step with you," Lucy said as

126

he lit a match and puffed heavily on his cigar. He threw the match into the fireplace and expending another perfect representation of a sperm in smoke, he said, "I'm glad to see you finally coming into your own."

Cassie shook her head. "Here we go again. I swear you guys are a match made in heaven. You both love to talk about me like I'm a freaking science experiment or something."

Lucy smirked again, the tips of his teeth emerging from his bottom lip, smoke streaming from his nostrils like a bull preparing to charge. "That's not so far from the truth," he said with a tilt of his head.

"What's that supposed to mean?" Cassie asked, leaning forward in her chair.

"Nothing," replied Lucy as he paused to puff at his cigar. He continued to stare at Cassie while he could see her mind trying to wrap around what he just implied. "I know it's hard to be patient with us. It is hard for me too sometimes. But, if nothing else, we are patient people," another pause to smirk and puff his cigar. "There are things in this world that though complex are capable of being understood. Take good and evil, for example. They are very complicated subjects indeed and have inspired years of thought and consideration among the brightest minds the world has ever known. The answer of 'What is good?' or 'What is evil?' may never be known. The parameters of the answer depend on what *is* known, *is* understood, and therefore we will have a better opportunity of understanding what the answer may be. However, there are some things that do not fall within such simple parameters, so to simply try and explain it, to simply say what it is, would not do *it* or *you* the justice it deserves." Lucy ended his soliloquy with another large puff of smoke; this one resembling a talk bubble in a comic strip.

Cassie imagined seeing the words 'There is no such thing as a bad PB&J' in it before it dissipated. She smiled and knowingly nodded her head. "You're talking about the Guardians, aren't you?"

"Very good," Lucy said with a smile.

"And so basically you're saying that you're not going to tell me who they are," Cassie said with a shrug.

Lucy leaned forward to extinguish his cigar. "Basically I'm telling you that I can't."

Cassie swallowed another 'Whatever' and instead just nodded her head.

"But what I will tell you," Lucy said with his hands on his knees, preparing to stand, "Is that the Guardians are neither good nor evil. They have one purpose, and they will execute it with immaculate precision."

"To save the garden," Cassie finished for him.

Lucy stood. "Yes, to save the garden."

Cassie shook her head. "Crapballs," she mumbled.

Lucy nodded his. "Yes, crapballs indeed."

The way he said it made Cassie laugh, but when she looked up he wasn't smiling, nor was he smirking, nor was he sneering. His mouth was closed so tight, the muscles of his jaw twitched, and there was something like sadness in his eyes. It was a familiar look Cassie could remember from her mirror. It was how her father looked those nights when he would stand in her doorway before he was about to leave again. It was not something she would normally analyze, but she continued to think about it anyway.

"Goodnight, Cassandra," he finally said, before he turned to the doors. With his back to her, she heard, "We've placed some of your father's work in your room. Study it well." And then he opened the door and was gone.

Cassie continued to sit there motionless trying to process everything she had just been told. It did not take long for her to realize how tired she was, or to remember what a long journey it would be to return to her room.

Slowly she stood up and left the stone room. She was not surprised to find Constance waiting for her at the foot of the stairs.

CHAPTER FIFTEEN - MOUSTACHE AND COFFEE

Nine books were laid out upon her bed, side-by-side as if nine parts of a body. Nine books bound in leather each with a large number scratched awkwardly into the cover. Nine leather-bound books ordered and numbered and laid out on her bed as if nine separate parts of a sleeping body were waiting for one to be removed so they all could be awakened; not as a body, nor as a book, but as the memory of her father.

She had seen these books before; all those nights as a child standing in the doorway of her father's study, wanting only for him to turn around and see her standing there in the doorway, but he never would because of these very books. She could be standing right next to him, staring at him and his head bent over the worn pages. Her father's fingers would be frantically working on filling every blank space the page allowed. She could be standing there forever and still he would not look up, not even when she said "Good night, daddy," and slowly made her way out of the room, never taking her eyes off of him, waiting for him to look up, to look at her, but he never did.

"Good night, baby," he would say as an afterthought, sometimes in a whisper and sometimes after she had already walked out of the room.

She hated these books because they took her father away from her. But she also loved these books because they were her father's and the only thing she had left of him. So it was with tears rolling down her cheeks that she slowly and carefully stacked them, starting with the one by her pillow, the one marked 'Nine', and ending with the first one at the foot of the bed.

Constance watched her do this from the doorway, listening to the quiet sobs from the tired girl. She would have held her; she would have told her that everything was going to be all right, but she knew that this was something Cassie had to go through alone. So she just stood there, and listened, and when Cassie was finished stacking the books, placing them on the nightstand beside the bed, she watched Cassie exhaustively climb under the covers.

"That's better," Constance whispered. Then she wished Cassie a good night even though it was almost morning. As she closed the door and less light was allowed into the room turning her body into darkness and shadow, Cassie was once again struck by her loss. She knew she would part with everything she did have for the one person she didn't have. Tears carried her into the realms of sleep.

A sense of loss and of being lost, of dark alleys in unknown cities, of shadows without substance, of children without fathers, of voices with no words filled Cassie's dreamscape. When Cassie lay waking a few hours later she felt as she had the morning after she found out her father was gone. Where Cassie's face had pressed into her pillow was the imprint of a mirror image face of salt water imprinted on her pillow. She felt as if a heavy hand was pressing down on the top of her head and holding her motionless.

Cassie sat up in bed. She blinked her eyes repeatedly until the residue of sleep had broken and her vision cleared. With her clear sight came remembrance of where she was, why she was where she was, and finally who she was.

A remnant of a dream caused Cassie to speak aloud, "My name is not Cassandra," she said while looking down at her hands. "It's Cassie." Then she opened her hands, lifted the blanket from her legs, and got out of bed.

Normally, the first thing she would do after waking up and getting out of bed was stretch, but she didn't. Cassie was certain that *this* morning was not the morning to do things the way she normally would. Consequently, she passed over her morning routine with one exception. She checked Frankie's bed to see if he was still asleep, but it had already been vacated, so she continued walking out of the room with her shoulders slumped and her head down. She felt like she had just woken from a very long strange dream. Cassie didn't raise her head as she walked down the hallway in order to avoid seeing *anything* to remind her that she hadn't.

In search of breakfast, Cassie thought she was having a truly bad hair day and it made her feel uncomfortable to be wearing the same clothes she had worn yesterday. On the negative side it seemed she could smell everything she had ever eaten in her life on her breath. Cassie didn't care. There was only one thing she wanted at the moment and she knew exactly where she needed to go to get it.

She could hear laughter coming from somewhere in the house,

perhaps the kitchen, which was her destination. It was honest laughter, not forced as it is when you're talking to someone you don't want to be talking to, or flirting with a boy who says something he thinks you would think would be funny. It was just someone laughing, just someone happy enough to make a spontaneous sound because of it. It sounded like her brother, and she hated the sound of it.

After her father died, the school psychologist told her that anger was a secondary emotion. She didn't understand it then. She thought she did, but she was too angry to understand anything then. Now, however, she thought she knew what the school psychologist meant.

The laughter got progressively louder as she made her way through the house. Finally she found its source. Standing in the doorway of the kitchen, Cassie saw Frankie, Max, and Key sitting at the kitchen table. All of them were laughing, but Frank was laughing the hardest. Willie was up on the table turning in circles between plates of pancakes and bowls of Cheerios.

"What's going on in here?" Cassie commanded from the doorway. "Do you have to make so much freaking noise?"

Everybody was laughing too hard to hear her. They didn't even realize that she was standing there until Frank, in a fit of laughter, nearly fell out of his chair.

"Oh, Cassie!" he said. "You have got to check this out." Turning to Key and pointing at him, his body still convulsing with laughter he said, "Do it again!"

"Okay, lady," Key said. "Watch this."

Key held out a Cheerio in front of him near where Willie was spinning in circles. In mid-spin, Willie noticed it and stopped, eagerly crawling towards Key's hand. She plucked the Cheerio with her pincers and returned to her position in the center of the table. The laughter around the table quieted down to chuckles in anticipation of what was about to happen. Willie seemed to be well aware of what was expected from her. She dropped the Cheerio in front of her, did a little hop on her eight legs, and quickly devoured the little circle of oaty goodness. Then she paused, as if in deep concentration.

"Here it comes!" Frank announced with his hands out.

A moment passed in silence in which all eyes stared at the puppy-sized spider on the table, and just when it seemed like nothing would happen, a shiver passed through Willie's body, beginning at her head and ending at the tip of her abdomen, and it was from there that a short, high-pitched squeak emerged.

The table once again erupted in laughter, which so pleased Willie that she again started to spin in circles, periodically emitting more of these little squeaks, occasionally stopping to produce a slightly longer, slightly deeper one.

"She's farting!" Frank tried to catch his breath long enough to say. "Cheerio farts!"

Cassie let a chuckle of her own out before she caught herself, to once again be reminded that there was nothing funny about the situation, even if the situation included a puppy-sized spider letting out Cheerio farts while spinning around in circles.

"It's not funny!" Cassie yelled at the boys while still standing in the doorway.

Frank turned to look at her as if she was crazy. "Are you kidding?" he asked, still out of breath. "Are you not seeing and hearing what she's doing?"

Even Max chimed in. "You have to admit, Cassie that this is farting funny!"

"Yeah, lady," Key added, slapping his hand on the table for effect. "She fart and fart, and I laugh and laugh. How come no laugh?"

"Cause it's not funny, Key!" Cassie said with a huff, stomping into the kitchen and turning from the scene at the table to search the counters. Had she looked any longer, an actual laugh might have escaped her mouth despite her iron demeanor. "Where's the coffee?" she continued with exasperation. "Isn't there any coffee in this place? I really need some coffee!"

Willie finally tired of her spinning and her farting, and crawled into Frank's lap. "Since when do you drink coffee?" he asked, petting the rough hairs of Willie's abdomen.

"Since I became the savior of the world," Cassie answered without turning around. She was too busy moving cooking jars around and opening and closing drawers in search of a coffeemaker or a way to make coffee. It was unlikely. She knew she would not find a coffeemaker hidden behind cooking jars or within drawers filled with silverware. "I swear I'm going to murder somebody if I don't get some coffee soon!" She slammed another drawer shut to punctuate her point and turned to the boys sitting at the table. She crossed her arms over her chest and answered their stares with a scowl.

"I guess she really wants some coffee," Max said as an aside to Frank.

"I guess so," Frank whispered back, never taking his eyes off his sister just in case she came at him with a rolling pin or an eggbeater.

"Hey Key, how about you go find Abigail before my sister spoons out our eyes with a melon-baller."

"Good idea!" Key said, sounding relieved to have an excuse to leave the room. He hopped out of his chair and quickly ran off.

Cassie continued to stare daggers at Frankie and Max.

Frankie and Max stared back, confused and a little scared.

Willie curled up into a ball in Frankie's lap, making strange sounds that Frank assumed was its version of a cat's purr. They sounded like the snipping scissors of a quick-working hair stylist.

"God, would you shut that thing up!" Cassie finally said.

Frank and Max simultaneously turned to each other to echo a mouthed 'Wow!' before turning slowly back to Cassie.

"Sheesh, Sis," Frank said, "what the heck happened to you last night? Did you see another shadow man?"

"No, I did not see another shadow man last night!" Cassie exclaimed, angrily uncrossing and re-crossing her arms over her chest.

"Then what did happen?" Max asked softly.

"Oh, nothing," Cassie said, "just more weirdness to add to the parade of weirdapalooza that is my life." She sighed and shook her head, turning from the boys to once again start a futile search for the coffee maker. "I swear to God if I don't get some freaking coffee…"

It was at that moment that Key entered the kitchen again, dragging Abigail by the apron, as Ms. Lonely purred contentedly in her arms.

"We need coffee, Abby, and quick! Nice lady going crazy," Key announced.

Cassie turned to find herself face to face with the reminder of the weirdness of a cat who did the talking for a woman. Ms. Lonely countered Cassie's angry stare with a meow and then a hiss.

Abigail, on the other hand, just smiled and nodded.

"Can I *please* have some coffee?" Cassie practically begged.

Abigail nodded her head again, and quickly moved into action, retrieving the coffeemaker from a cupboard that nobody had noticed before. Abigail also brought out a steel canister containing coffee beans, a coffee grinder, a metal creamer, a bowl of sugar, and even another of fresh ground cinnamon. The coffee was brewing faster than any of them could imagine possible, especially with all the various things needed around the kitchen to make it happen. But even given the haste of Abigail's work, Cassie still stood there stoically, with her arms crossed over her chest and a foot tapping out a rhythm matched by the brewing percolations.

Finally a cup of coffee was produced and placed on the counter by Abigail. Ms. Lonely hopped from Abby's arms onto the counter. She pushed the creamer with her head towards Cassie, who had already picked up the cup of the dark, hot brew.

"I take it black," Cassie pointedly said to Ms. Lonely.

"Yeah, just like her shadow men," came from Frank snickering in the background.

"Shut up, Frank!" Cassie said after an exorcist-like turning of her head toward the table. She turned back to face Abigail to thank her for the coffee before stomping to the kitchen table holding her coffee. Cassie sat with a huff.

The first sip caused a reaction on Cassie's face as if she had just eaten a lemon and she had to suppress the urge to spit it back into the cup. Her face turned red, her eyes watered, and a tiny cough emerged from Cassie's throat after she forced herself to swallow the mouthful of coffee. After a moment to recover, she put the cup back on the table, sat back in her chair, and sighed. "Ahhh. Now that's a good cuppa Joe!"

Frankie and Max looked on trying to contain their laughter, but the last line was too much, even for them, and they couldn't hold it in any longer. Abigail and Key, who had been looking on from the kitchen counter joined in; Abigail silently laughing with a hand over her mouth and shudders quivering through her entire body; Key with tears in his eyes, holding his stomach with one hand and slapping his knee with the other. Even Ms. Lonely appreciated the absurdity of it all and purred contentedly, her tail stiffening and shaking as if it was laughing too.

Cassie tried to resist. She tried to maintain that stoic, dour demeanor, but she couldn't. Slowly her features softened and soon she was laughing just as hard as the rest of them.

Finally the laughter died down. Abigail replaced all the coffee making materials while Ms. Lonely watched her from the counter. Key took his place at the kitchen table, crossing his arms on the table and leaning his head on them. He seemed to have more than just a casual interest in Cassie and watched as she continued to sip her coffee, laughing to himself when she reacted to every sip with a "Blech!" Frank and Max also relaxed. Frankie returned his attention to Willie in his lap, while Max went back to eating his pancakes.

Abigail finished putting everything away, and after scooping up Ms. Lonely in her large, generous arms, she made her way out of the kitchen with a nod and a smile to everyone at the table.

"Where are Ryan and Kyle?" Cassie asked between 'blechs'.

"They're outside in the garden," Frank said. He was still looking down at Willie in his lap as he petted her.

"Yeah, you could almost say they were guarding it," Max added.

Frank looked up so he could nod his head at Max. "I guess you could kind of call them Guardians, huh?"

"I guess so!" Max said with a smirk and a quick glance to make sure Cassie was smiling, which she was. "Except, as Guardians," he continued, "Ryan and Kyle would not destroy the world; they love Taco Bell too much!"

"Of course," Frank agreed, the smile on his face widening until both of them broke out into laughter.

Cassie was laughing too, though she was trying not to. "Would you guys shut up? It isn't funny."

"What *Taco Bell*?" Key asked confused.

"Nothing, Key," Cassie replied kindly. "It's just some stupid fast food place back in America."

"Taco Bell is not stupid!" Frank insisted. "Don't listen to her, Key."

Key lifted his head from his arms and looked back and forth between Frank and Cassie, wondering who to believe. Finally his eyes settled on Cassie. "Nice lady right. Taco Bell stupid," he said before resting his head on his arms again.

"Thank you, Key," Cassie said with a nod and a smile, ignoring the "Whatever" that came from Frank.

Max looked on in obvious delight, especially at the way Key was watching Cassie, which reminded him of how he himself watched

Cassie. "So," he finally said after the Taco Bell debate had ended, "what happened last night? Why were you so grumpy earlier?"

Cassie looked daggers at Frank. "You didn't tell him?"

Frank refused to meet his sister's stare. "Sorry, I got distracted."

"Distracted by what?"

Frank shook his head as if it was obvious why he was distracted and he responded, "Um, the spinning and the farting Cheerios beast?"

"Whatever," Cassie said before turning to Max. "I met Constance's husband last night."

"No way!" Max said impressed. "For some reason I never imagined Constance as being married."

"Me either," Cassie agreed.

"So what was he like?" Max continued. "Was he weird? Was he all Constance-y? Did he say things that didn't make sense?"

Cassie nodded her head at each subsequent question. "Yes, yes and more yes. He's different though, like a different kind of weird." Cassie thought about it for a second, letting her head fill with the image of Lucy's face in the fire's light. "I don't know. It was almost like I knew him already or something. As if I liked him or something, or thought that I was supposed to like him. I don't know. It's hard to explain. Plus, and this is going to sound really weird, but his name is Lucy."

"*Lucy?*" Frank and Max asked in unison.

"Yeah," Cassie said with a laugh, "isn't that weird?"

"Totally," Max said, nodding his head, not sure how he felt about the way Cassie talked about liking Lucy.

"Did he have a moustache?" Frank asked.

Cassie shook her head. She did not expect such a question nor did she understand why he would even ask, but it was her brother after all, and she was used to Frank asking questions nobody else would think to ask. "No, Frank, he didn't have a moustache."

"Well, what kind of a moustache would he have if he had a moustache?" was the follow-up question.

Cassie shook her head harder, this time with her eyes closed. "I'm sorry... *what*?"

Frank turned to Max for support before returning his attention to his sister. "I mean if he did wear a moustache, what kind of moustache would it be?"

"Yeah, Frank, I understood the question," Cassie said. "I just don't understand why you would ask it."

"I want to know because a moustache says a lot about a man. Like if he had a Yosemite Sam, it would mean he's kind of a hot head. If it was a Fu Man Chu, it would mean he's kind of mysterious and you really don't know if you can trust him or not."

"Right! I get it," Max said to Cassie, covering his mouth trying to hide his smile. "Like if he had a Johnny Depp it means he's a pirate."

"Exactly!" Frank said, with no smile to have to hide.

All Cassie could do was stare incredulously at the back of Frankie's head and wonder if he was actually her brother. "Frank," she said.

"Yeah?" he answered.

"You're an idiot."

Now there was a smile, and he wasn't hiding it. "Thank you," he said.

"So what did he say?" Max asked, trying to change the subject

KENNY FIGULY & LENNA FIGULY

away from moustaches.

Cassie shrugged her shoulders. "Eh, a bunch of stuff that didn't make much sense, just like everybody else around here. But, when I got back to my room there were nine journals of dad's on my bed. How cool is that?"

"*Really*?" Frank said, perking up at the mention of their father.

"Totally!" Cassie answered.

And just like that, Frank was out of his chair, forgetting that Willie was in his lap. She clicked annoyingly after falling to the floor. "Sorry, Willie," Frank said with a frown, before turning back to his sister. "What are we waiting for? Let's go check them out!"

He was already hurrying out of the kitchen before Cassie could respond. She felt sick to her stomach and she had what seemed to be a fist sized rock in her throat. Max could sense that something was wrong, especially since Cassie had yet to move from her chair. He swallowed hard. He put his hand over hers. He waited until she looked up at him to say, "You know you don't have to do this alone."

The way Max was looking at her made her want to cry. "I know I don't," she said; not believing herself but *wishing* she could. She dared not to look Max in the eyes and have him see her lie, so she simply kept her eyes down and said, "Thank you," as one loving friend to another.

They both stood and slowly left the kitchen, neither one realizing that Key had fallen asleep at the table until after they had left him alone in the room.

Max was the one who volunteered to return to the kitchen to wake him.

CHAPTER SIXTEEN - NINE BOOKS OF OLD BONES

"I have old bones. The sun sets over the sand and the shadows rise in its wake. It is true; they are real. What have I done?"

Frank was sitting on Cassie's bed; Key leaned in close beside him, following the words with a forefinger like a child being read a bedtime story; and though Frank had stopped reading, his lips continued to twitch. Finally, he looked up at Cassie and Max who were still standing in the doorway. He shook his head. His eyes widened then narrowed. His mouth was still open.

Cassie looked back at him. She knew what he was thinking. All those years their father was alive he was more like a ghost than a man. Every once in a while he would appear in the house, hovering from room to room, distant and distracted, his glasses so low down the bridge of his nose that the slightest movement would cause them to fall. His hair was always a mess upon his head from the constant scratching and ruffling of the hand that was not holding a pen. And books upon books were everywhere when he was haunting his study. There were books on the desk, books on the floor, books on his tiny brown couch, and books in his lap. Each was open upon another, and then another, as he pored over them, pen in his hand.

But other times, when he didn't have that look in his eye, like the faraway flame of a candle in the darkest of nights, he was more like a god than a ghost. He was ever present, calm and patient, but always quick to express his love. Sometimes he would sneak up behind Cassie or Frank to startle them with a hug, or to hold them so tight and lift them so high that only fits of laughter could describe how it made them feel. Sometimes he would look at them and there was no darkness in his eyes at all, only light, like looking at the sun reflected on calm waters. Perhaps it was because he would sometimes look at them. With tears in his eyes, tears that he wished weren't there, which is why, like his glasses, they would never fall. And it was these moments however few, when their father was everything they could ever want him to be and more. That made all the other distracted moments much harder. It made them miss him even more when he was gone; whether gone from the house or within it like a ghost.

And now this was all that was left of him, these books. The books they hated so much while growing up they blamed them for taking their father away from them. The books they were never allowed to read. The books that now were all open upon the bed. Reading them caused Cassie to understand the expression on her brother's face. His face and eyes held laughter and crying, complete joy and pleading despair. It was as if reading the books answered the most important question of his life with a better question. It was at that moment that she realized that no matter what else happened, no matter what else was in store for her, there was somebody in her life who would always understand her, even just by something as simple as the look on her face.

Frankie seemed to have realized this too, because they were now smiling at each other, despite the tears that refused to fall from their eyes.

Max did not want to disturb the moment. He could only imagine what this must be like for Cassie and Frankie. His father was like a ghost to him too, but at least he was still alive. There was hope that one day things might be different; at least there was still a possibility that they might be. So he did not say anything, and quietly made his way to Cassie's bed. He sat down on the edge of it, placed one of the books in his lap, opened it, read a little, shook his head and closed the book to look at its cover. He picked another book and did the same thing with it; and then another, going through the motions faster and faster with each new book. The expression on his facial expression growing more and more confused. Max was scrunching his eyes and his lips up tighter and tighter. Finally, when he finished with the last book, he looked up, barely able to see anything through the tiny slit in his eyelids.

Cassie was now on the bed too, hugging Frankie from his side. Frankie still had the open book in his lap and did not turn all the way towards Cassie to hug her back with his available arm. On the other side of him, Key had stood and was hugging him around the neck, so that both Cassie's and Key's heads seemed to sprout from Frankie's shoulders. Certainly an odd thing to see for Max, and if it wasn't for the odd thing that came before it, he would have surely made some sort of smartass comment. But instead, he just said, "Um… guys?"

All three of them also had their eyes closed, and they all opened them at the same time. Then they disengaged from each other, Key crawling uncomfortably over Frankie's lap in order to sit in Cassie's. Finally Frank coughed and said, "What's up?"

"Um..." Max began, not sure how to begin. "Well..." still not sure. "Um..."

Cassie wiped her eyes and smiled at the look on Max's face.

"Just spit it out, Max," she said to him.

"Max!" Key echoed while covering his face with his hands. "Just spit it!"

"Well," Max tried again. "Your dad...um...wasn't...you know..."

"Wasn't a leprechaun?" Frank finished for him. "No, he wasn't a leprechaun."

Max shook his head and unschrunched his eyes. "No...I mean...he was alright, right?"

Cassie turned to Frank with a look of indignation. "I think he's asking if dad was crazy." She turned back to Max, this time with a look on her face that immediately caused Max to inch further away from her on the bed. "You're not asking if our dad was crazy, are you? Cause I can't think of anything *craaazzzzier* than calling my dad crazy. Can you think of anything that *craaazzzy*, Frank? I mean, he couldn't be that *craaazzzy*, could he?"

Frank and Max quickly glanced at each. "Um, actually Cassie," Frank began. "Saying crazy that many times in a row makes you sound a little crazy. Oops, I mean *craaazzzy*."

"Shut up, Frank," Cassie said, turning quickly to him before narrowing her eyes at Max again.

"You guys funny!" Key added, looking up at Cassie's face, before

146

turning back to Max to lean forward and whisper, "And a little crazy too."

Max closed his eyes and shook his head. "No, that's not what I meant. Well, I guess it was what I meant but just listen." He grabbed one of the books, opened it and started reading. "I have old bones. They came again last night just like he said they would. Have you forsaken me? Or have you forgiven me?" Then he closed the book and held it out for the others to see the cover. "It's called the Third Map." He put it down and picked up another. "This is the Fifth Map," opening it and again reading the first page. "I have old bones. He warned me not to enter. But I had no choice. The siege had ended and they were coming from the east. When I entered the tower the bodies filled every room and I could see the darkness in their eyes." Max closed the book and put it down while shaking his head. "I mean, they all start that way. 'I have old bones.' I just don't understand how your dad...I mean...what the hell was he trying to say? And how could he know some of this stuff? Like that last one, I was reading more of it before and I remember we learned about some of it in History. It's from the *First Crusade,* the Siege of *Antioch*, and the Tower of the *Two Sisters*. The 'they' he was talking about that were coming from the east, well, that was the Muslim army."

For some reason, Cassie had been afraid to look at the books herself. They were the last thing she had left from her father and somehow opening the books meant that he was really gone. But now her curiosity had gotten the best of her and she grabbed one and opened it in Key's lap since he was sitting in her own.

The smell of the paper and the leather is what struck her first. It smelled like that room she had hated so much as a child. It smelled of the room she would stand by the door of at night after Frankie had gone asleep. It was a room that seemed to hold her father like it was a prison, allowing nothing more than a narrow view of him from the slight space from the door left ajar; the slight space between prison bars. The next thing that struck her about her father as she secretly watched him was his handwriting, and she thought it might be too much to bear. The letters were sometimes sturdy as if he was concentrating very hard on how they looked, but at other times, they seemed more frantic and haphazard as if his hand could not move fast enough to write them down. She took a deep breath and shook her head, flipping through the pages with her eyes out of focus. "So much time," she mused. "A whole lifetime," she thought. "And this is all that is left."

Key reached his little hand out so it was caught between the flipping pages, stopping them. He turned the pages back to where his hand rested. He looked back up at Cassie and without saying anything, tapped his finger on the book. Then he turned back around.

Cassie refocused her eyes. Cassie read.

It came again last night. I knew it would, and though the moment terrified me, I knew I wanted it to come. I had to know why. I had to know why me?

I did not move when it first appeared, rising from the darkness in the corner of the room, tall and thin, and that smell, that sweet smell of rotting flesh; I could not move. I had to know.

It stood there, staring at me. I could feel its eyes though I could not see them. They were like a shadow created not from light, but from the absence of it. Darkness holds no weight but this thing, this thing that stood there and stared at me. Was this thing their father had known and been able to describe in such detail the exact thing she had experienced? How could someone else experience the same experience she had gone through in the first place? What the hell was her father trying to tell her? And, most importantly, did he know this was going to happen to her?

Cassie leaned her head back against the wall, closed her eyes and shook her head. She could not believe that he knew. She could not believe that he wouldn't tell her. She could not believe he wouldn't say something to her. She could not believe that he would leave her all alone.

She banged the back of her head against the wall, not hard, just hard enough to rattle her thoughts away. Then she bit her lip and said in a whisper, "I don't understand."

She felt Key's tiny hand on her arm. She opened her eyes to see him looking back at her, a straight line of a smile on his little face, looking as if he understood exactly what she was thinking. When their eyes met, his smile grew. "Poppa no crazy, lady," he said. "Poppa very smart man. He knew, now you know, and soon we all know. Very smart man, lady. Very smart." Key nodded his head definitively, and then turned back around to the book.

Cassie laughed to herself. Then she put her arms around little Key and squeezed him as tight as she could. A muffled, "Smart and strong!" emerged from the hug.

Frankie and Max were still arguing about who did better sophomore year in History, so Cassie interrupted them with a "Guys."

Frank was still in the mood to argue however. "Don't even start, Cass. You always hated History!"

Cassie rolled her eyes. "Um, guys. I think I figured something out," she said plainly.

Max leaned forward. "Oh yeah?" he asked.

"Yeah," she said. "I don't think this is the first time this has happened. I think that's what all these books are about, other times like this. I just read this whole passage describing exactly the same thing that happened to me that night at the hostel. I think that's what dad had been researching the whole time. I think this was his way of trying to... to help, you know?" She had to say the last part while looking down, because she was afraid that if she met any of their eyes when she said it, her eyes welling with tears would spill over until she was crying.

"Huh," Frank said. Max, however, still did not understand.

"But that still doesn't explain how he could have known this stuff. If he was just trying to explain all this cra..." He stopped before getting out the word craziness again. "I mean all this stuff. Why wouldn't he just come out and say it. Why does everything have to be so backward?"

Cassie shrugged her shoulders and looked imploringly at Max, but when she spoke it was plainly and calmly. "I don't know, Max. I mean, I can't tell you that. I hardly even knew my father so I can't tell you why he would do the things he did. But there was a reason why he wrote these books. There is a reason why we have them, just like there is a reason why this is all happening. What we need to do now is figure it out."

Max considered what he just heard for a moment, looking down at the open book in his lap and pinching his bottom lip. Then he looked up at Cassie and said, "You know, that's the first thing that's made any sense to me in a long, long time."

Cassie's smile dimpled her cheeks. "Thanks, Maxie!"

Max's cheeks turned red and he awkwardly looked back down at the book in his lap.

Frank rolled his eyes at this little exchange and was thankful when Kyle and Ryan appeared in the doorway. Both of them were flushed and sweaty and seemed out of breath.

"Hey, guys," Kyle said, making his way to the other bed and dropping heavily onto it. "You know they have a basketball court out there. God, Constance has a mean jump shot! You guys should come and play."

Frank snorted and sarcastically said, "Um, yeah, well, we're a little busy saving the world and all, but maybe when we're done."

Kyle ignored him. "Constance really is good. That woman can play some ball! She says she's always kicking her husband's ass."

Cassie laughed and watched as Ryan came over to their bed and curiously looked at the books. "I doubt she said it like that," Cassie said with a smirk to Kyle.

Ryan was the one who answered her though. "No, it was more like this," he said, straightening his back, holding his chin up and taking on the air of being prim and proper. He spoke in a higher voice with something of a poorly done English accent. "Winning and losing is purely a matter of perspective. Often the one who wins has lost something in return, something, which perhaps amounts to more than the victory. And often the one who loses has gained more than they could ever know. Only time can decide such a thing." Raising his voice even higher, "In the context of my husband and basketball I have always been and always will be the victor."

They all laughed at his impression with Key laughing the hardest and slapped his knee. Ryan turned even redder and sweated even harder than he was before. When the laughter finally died down, he asked what they were doing in order to turn their attention away from him.

"These are all my dad's journals," Cassie said. "We think they have something to do with what's been happening."

Ryan picked one of them up and looked at the cover. "The Seventh Map?" he said. He opened the book, his eyes squinting. "Doesn't look like a map."

Kyle stood and looked at the book he had opened too. "It just looks like a book to me, Cass."

Frank shook his head annoyed. "Well, my dad called them Maps for a reason," he said pointedly. "Obviously they've got to lead us somewhere."

Ryan shook his head for another reason. His first impulse was to say nothing. Whenever he had a differing opinion from somebody else, he always assumed it was wrong. But this time, he was pretty sure he was right. "I think maybe you're thinking about it in the wrong way," he said somewhat meekly.

Cassie looked up at him with a curious twinkle in her eye. "What do you mean?" she asked.

Ryan's confidence was buoyed by her interest in what he had to say and he continued. "Well, I think you're imagining the word map as if it was a treasure map or something; like if you follow it, it'll lead you somewhere." He swallowed hard before he continued, as he was about to come to the point he was trying to make. "But maybe they're just more like road maps. Maybe they're just showing all the different directions you can go. Maybe they're not supposed to *lead* you somewhere, but just show you where people have gone before, you know?" Ryan stopped to notice all the eyes now on him, turning him red again with embarrassment. He shrugged his shoulders and finished with, "Or maybe I have no idea what I'm talking about."

They all sat in silence for a moment, just looking at him. Finally Max said, "I don't think you were doing an impersonation of Constance. I think you *are* Constance."

They all laughed again, except for Cassie. She was looking down at the book, feeling the worn pages between her fingers.

Key looked back up at her, that flat smile on his face again. "He very smart man too," he whispered.

Cassie smiled back at him. Then she ruffled his hair with one of her hands before kissing him on the top of his head.

CHAPTER 17 - DREAMLAND

There were memories here. Was she awake or asleep? They didn't make sense but somehow they belonged to her. She looked to her right to see her brother asleep on the bed across from her as moonlight glimmered into the center of the room. There was also movement, a hushed movement that carried with it something recognizable and dark. Cassie needed to see more and sat up in bed, surveying the room. At the base of the bedroom door was a large figure dressed in black, kneeling in prayer. For reasons she didn't understand the figure felt nonviolent.

"Hello," she whispered.

The figure in black stood and walked to her bedside. It was Lucifer. He didn't enter the conversation with his usual sarcasm. He smiled. A perfect row of teeth showed with a faint hint of happiness.

"You're losing faith, my dear Cassie." He lit a cigarette and slowly exhaled. The smoke was thin and blue. The smell of cloves filled the vacant air.

"I'm tired."

"I'm certain you mean tired of this experience."

"Wouldn't you be?"

"Cassie I live for the chase. Your problem is that you have so little to go by. I suppose it's time for a true and faithful explanation"

Cassie yawned. "That would be nice."

"The books are holding you down. Am I warm?" He smiled again. This time when he smiled his teeth conveyed a sense of foreboding.

"You don't always have to be so damn scary." Cassie giggled at her own reproach.

"I like your style Cassie."

"I'd like to think of myself as a forward thinker. After all, I am having a conversation with the devil."

"That's true," he mused, as if he were heavy in thought.

"So we're going to talk straight this time?"

"What would you like to know?"

"Where is this conversation leading me; leading all of us?" She turned on the bed to face him directly. He was heavy in thought, taking another drag off of his clove cigarette.

"Cassie, the books aren't just scribbling's of a mad man. Although I must admit your father walked close to the edge at times, he was solid in his thoughts."

"I don't know what that means."

"There are pictures that represent places and definitions of times and events no other human could comprehend."

"Why choose him? Why my father? Was he different?" Cassie felt tears welling up inside of her. She refused to let them fall and lead her to fall prey to her own weaknesses.

"No one chose your father, Cassie. He allowed himself to dig deep. There are certain things mortal men should never know. He found those things and pursued them with a passion unmatched by any other."

"Was he crazy?"

"In what way does that make him crazy? Your father was far from crazy. He was and still is very solid in his thinking."

"He's alive?"

"In many ways, yes he is."

"He's alive in many ways? What's that supposed to mean?" Cassie allowed her anger to show.

"Cassie, he's alive. I'm just not sure the Guardians will allow him to ever see the light of day."

"This is because of his knowledge of them?"

"That's correct."

"That's shit!" Cassie spat out.

"That's why your job is so important. You must find the Guardians and convince them the world of man is worth saving. They have blasphemed their own existence. There is nothing worthy of their survival left."

"That doesn't make sense," Cassie spoke her thoughts aloud.

"If it makes so little sense to you then it's your job to come up with a viable argument against the truth."

"I'm just a girl."

"You are the daughter of hope. A lot of people are counting on your insight."

"I don't know where to begin."

"Have you given an honest attempt at reading those journals?"

Just as the devil had finished his sentence, one of the journals appeared on the bed beside her.

"To hell with that," spat Cassie.

"Exactly," he said with a grin.

Satan pointed to the center of the room. A puff of smoke swooshed to life, revealing a small impish looking creature with large, yellow eyes and a pointy hat. His arms were filled with the remaining eight journals. Once again, Cassie felt no fear. Was she actually getting used to the peculiar happenings?

The creature walked over to her, laying the books at her feet.

"These are for you, my dear," it said.

"Thank you," said Cassie with apprehension.

The imp winked at Satan and sat down on the ground. Several more of the same creatures popped up and took their respective spots on the floor. Cassie caught herself admiring their clothes. They were tightly fitted leather with green and black kimonos. Their eyes looked playful, even mischievous. Cassie found them far more interesting than disturbing. In a way, she was proud of her own composure, considering the situation and present company.

"Those books represent salvation," said Lucifer considering the journals. The matter-of-fact tone within his voice was disconcerting.

"So let me get this straight. It's my job to prepare an argument for the salvation of the entire human race?" She laughed out loud helplessly. "I don't even know how to find the 'beings' that I'm supposed to address? This is nuts!"

"Oh, I totally agree," smiled Satan.

"That doesn't help."

"I'm only being honest with you, Cassie."

One of the squishy faced little imps jumped onto the bed and gave Cassie a hug. She was both repulsed and delighted at the same time. The inquisitive little creature ignored her obvious hesitation.

"Cassie you have the answers," said Satan.

"I don't have anything but questions!"

"You assume so much."

"I assume nothing," she said, feeling irritable. "You hate answering questions. Everything is always indirect with you. How the hell can you expect me to get anything out of our little talks when all you do is talk in riddles?"

Satan could hardly contain his own laughter. "You don't ask the right questions, Cassie. Pick up one of those books and look at it. Don't forget to leave out your emotions regarding your father. It's your emotions that cloud the meaning. Fear of learning the truth keeps you from finding it." Lucifer moved from the bedside and walked to the window, peering out into the darkness. Cassie felt his love for the unknown. But he knew. He knew more than he was letting on and the prospect of this knowledge was frustrating.

"This isn't helping me to understand."

"The things we create make up who we are."

"You're speaking in riddles again!"

"You, my dear Cassie, created a world in which your father has become more of a challenge than the answers that present themselves within those journals."

"So, it's my fault?" she sat horrified by the accusation.

"Exactly."

"That's crap!" Cassie countered.

"No, that's true. Your make believe little world has stopped you from seeing the obvious."

"Give me one example," she said, defiance filling her voice.

"Now is a perfect example. You're more interested in a conversation to save face than you are about those journals." He moved from the window to face her. Frankie mumbled something incoherent in his sleep and rolled over. Lucifer pointed in his direction.

"Frankie has nothing to do with anything," she snapped.

"That's because you don't trust him enough to allow him to express his ideas."

"Why would you say that? I love Frank. I tell him everything."

"You forget who you are talking to." Lucifer picked up the robe that was hanging over the mirror near the window and tossed it to Cassie. She put it on.

"Are we going somewhere?" she wondered.

"Yes."

"Are you going to tell me where, or is this a mystery as well?"

One of the imps, who'd previously been picking his nose, picked up a journal and handed it to Cassie. His finger was stuck in a specific page. She read the entry. After several seconds she looked up at Lucifer.

"I get it," she said, her heart pounding hard in her chest. "These aren't just words and pictures on a page. These are keys to the future. They point in a direction of choices." Cassie was ecstatic with her discovery. "This is a glimpse into history!" Cassie threw the book on the bed and picked up another from the pile, flipping each page with increasing enthusiasm. The imps began doing a jig, dancing back and forth around the bed.

"It's always been there, my dear." Lucifer waved his hand over the room and the imps vanished just as quickly as they appeared.

A mystery was revealed. Cassie had a new hold on the situation. Fear was replaced with knowledge.

"How quickly darkness turns to light when you're searching with open eyes," said Lucifer. He smiled that merciless. She hated him for that. His arrogance was unforgiving and crude.

"I've asked you the same questions before. I don't understand why you've..."

"I have given you every chance," he said, interrupting her.

"I'm not that weak!" retorted Cassie.

"There are no accusations here, sweetheart."

"It's hard to understand you," she replied, hating the defeat in her own voice. He'd made her sound stupid. In what way she wasn't sure; but it was there no matter how much he denied it. His words only made her tension greater than it had been.

Lucifer walked to the edge of the bedroom and opened the door. A flash of light flooded the room, blinding her momentarily. Within that very instant she was sitting up in her bed as light from the midday sun filled the room. Was it a dream? She looked over to see if her brother was still asleep in his bed. The bed was empty and it had been neatly made.

Cassie put on her robe and walked downstairs into the great room. Everyone was there neatly seated on the floor in front of a large screen television, playing X-Box. For some reason, the scene was more surreal than the dream she'd just came from.

"So this is how it works," she started. "I sleep half the day away and find out you guys have been playing games all morning. Gee whiz!" She sat down on the chair nearest Max. He had his back to her but motioned that he was aware of her presence.

"Hey, sis," Frank chimed in.

"Duke Nukem forever," cried Ryan, his fingers hammering the controller with a vengeance.

Cassie couldn't believe they'd come this far, practically the other side of the world, and the guys still found a way to play their juvenile games.

"Boys suck!" said Cassie, hoping they'd acknowledge her.

Max suddenly stood up and threw his controller at the back of Frankie's head.

"What's your deal?" said Frankie rubbing his head where the controller had connected.

"You know all the cheats. That's not even cool. We're on the same team, butt hole!" Max walked out of the room in a huff.

"He's a poor sport. I should kick his ass for that," said Frank. He stood up and clicked off the game. "From now on we play without him."

Willie cuddled up to Frankie's side and nuzzled Frankie's right leg in support. The spider was obviously irritated on Frank's behalf. Frankie leaned down and patted Willie on the head. "It's okay," said Frank. "We love Max even if he is a dick sometimes."

"Ha, ha, ha," laughed Key. "You called Max a dick. I know what a dick is. What a strange expression. I have one of those." Key repeated

161

the word several times as if proud of his new word discovery.

It was then that Constance entered the room. Her expression was both amused and dismayed. "What are you guys teaching the locals?" She smiled, winking at Frank.

"My brother is practicing to be a great educator someday," said Cassie.

"Frankie? Can Cassie be a dick? She's a girl", asked Key. "Girls don't have that."

"You are absolutely correct on that one, Key," said Constance. "I think we should refrain from using vulgar language in good company."

Key wasn't quite sure what Constance meant but he got the gist, deciding sadly that the dick word was something he shouldn't say.

Shortly thereafter Max entered the room, eyeballing Frank to see if there would be any retaliation. When he was sure of his safety he apologized. Frank just nodded his head and continued to rub the back of his head even though the pain was long gone.

Constance cleared her throat, gaining everyone's attention, including Willie. "My husband and I have to speak with you." She sat down on the chair nearest the massive fireplace and crossed her legs. She motioned for everyone to sit around her as they waited for Lucy to enter. To everyone's surprise, Lucy arrived with two large Bengal tigers at his side. Strangely, she was more fascinated to hear they were conversing with Lucy as they entered. The conversation had something to do about the economy in South Africa and how it was affecting the world diamond market.

"Now I've seen and heard everything," whispered Ryan into Frankie's ear. "What the heck?"

Lucy sat down next to his wife in the massive King Edward style throne as the two tigers sat on either side. The tigers began to argue quietly between themselves but were quickly hushed by a wave of Lucy's hand.

"First I'd like to introduce you to Tic and Tac," began Lucy. "They are my trusted guardians and my part time debate team." Lucy followed with a deep throaty laugh. Both tigers reared their heads and executed courtly bows.

"My husband wants to explain the journey you are all about to take," said Constance, leaning forward to make her point. Everyone fell silent.

Lucy took a deep breath. He examined everyone in the room, settling his eyes on Cassie. "Cassie had a revelation last night regarding her father's journals," he began. The group was still. Cassie was perplexed as to how Lucy knew of the dreams. She decided to say nothing in spite of her curiosity.

CHAPTER 18 - A PREPARATORY LESSON

Lucy spoke of the Tomb of the Prophets, of Haggai, Malachi and Zechariah. He spoke about The Well of Souls, under the Dome of the Rock where the dead meet twice a month to pray; not a tomb, but a sacred place in history. These places were markers, as explained in Professor Lint's journals. They demonstrated religion, culture and a mask that hid years of war and insurrection. His words fell like fire and ice. They were matter of fact and full of motion.

Cassie could tell he liked hearing himself speak of what he knew and how these places... these events affected humanity. These were not just places in time but maps in history. They pointed the way into another element of reality. It was there they had to go. They had to enter and find the ancient Guardians of the Earth; to entertain the nine beings responsible for the ultimate verdict of the continuance of humanity upon the planet. They were not gods but they held the knowledge of balance between the good of humanity that grew in the Garden and the evil of humanity that could destroy it.

Cassie was scared. She didn't want the responsibility. In a strange, detached sort of way, she went through the motions in her mind of what she would do to accomplish the task. She would face it head on, thinking only about the end result. She wouldn't allow herself the opportunity to wallow in the past. She refused to believe that the task could not be carried out. This new found strength gave her the fortitude to believe in the affirmative. These charges would be brought to the Guardians and argued with righteous endeavor.

"I would like to end this conversation with a warning," said Lucy, his eyes wide and serious. "You may not all survive this journey. I have seen the future and it is an indefinite path."

Everyone fell silent. They looked around at each other for support, knowing that it may be the last time they'd ever see each other under the shelter of protection again.

Lucy rose to leave the room. Tic and Tac did the same. He glanced down at everyone, smiling as he walked away. It was then that Cassie realized who Lucy truly was. Her blood ran cold. It was in the smile. Lucy was the man from her dreams. Lucy was Lucifer.

"Clever girl," he said in passing. Cassie didn't even raise her eyes to meet his. She gazed straight ahead, pretending it didn't matter. She was aware of his knowing the truth regarding her thoughts. She felt betrayed and embarrassed all at the same time.

"Who could she trust; certainly not this man?"

"And who was Constance?"

Cassie glanced over at Constance to see if she was watching. She was. Her look was one of genuine concern. Cassie wanted to believe in her. She had to. Without Constance they were stuck on an island in the middle of the desert.

"All of us have a part to play in this, dear," Said Constance. "All of us are seeking equilibrium. You must know that Cassie." Constance sat forward to emphasize her point. Everyone turned to Cassie in need of reassurance. It was obvious that Cassie and Constance were having a private conversation.

"Have you been lying to me... to us?" Tears welled up in Cassie's eyes. Her accusation was sharp. No one said a word until Constance chimed in.

"What does your heart tell you Cassie?"

"You tell me," said Cassie with cutting insolence. Constance wasn't reactionary. She responded with grace and understanding.

"I can't do that for you. I can tell you to look deeper than you have. You feel cheated because information was withheld from you." Constance sat back further into the chair, relaxing her body language. "I apologize to you, love. You deserve more. You have a strong heart and can be trusted. Lucy, or Lucifer, is my husband. And yes he visits you in your dreams to guide you. That's his way of communicating. He's rather indirect that way. I don't necessarily approve of it but it's how he does things."

"So who are you Constance?" asked Ryan, out of the blue. Kyle and Frankie squirmed nervously at Ryan's question. Max buried his head in his hands.

"I think the children are nervous," said a small, mousy looking creature that had propped itself upon Constance's shoulder. At this point all bets were off. No one was shocked. Constance gave the creature a peck on the cheek and then dismissed it. The creature, looking slightly disenchanted, scurried down the arm of her chair and disappeared.

"Some call me Gaia, an ancient immortal within the Greek pantheon and considered a Mother Titan or Mother Earth to be precise. My work is to preserve order over the living planet. Once again, much the same way my husband has explained himself to you, I am all about balance. Most who know me simply call me Mother." She cleared her throat. "Perhaps Mother Nature fits your awareness with more clarity."

"It makes sense to me," said Cassie. "This whole crazy thing is starting to make total sense." Cassie thought for a second, trying to clear her mind enough to find the words to articulate her new found interest.

"I'm lost," said Max, flabbergasted by the latest revelation. Yet he smiled, shaking his head in thankful relief. Just the sound of the word mother made his heart feel at ease.

"Why did you wait so long to tell us?" asked Cassie."

"Cassie," spoke Constance, "Would you have believed me had I revealed myself when we first met?"

"Perhaps not, I suppose."

"There's your answer," replied Constance. "Cassie, you and the others needed time to absorb all of the information. That's why Key brought you here. We needed to know what your fears and aspirations were before sending you on this journey."

"What would have happened if we didn't believe?" asked Kyle.

"Then Cassie would have failed and mankind would have died off."

"So you weren't sure if we would make it this far?" asked Cassie.

"I never doubted you for a second, my dear."

"When do we get started?" asked Kyle.

"That's the golden question," said Constance. "I think you're ready now. The fact of the matter is we are all running out of time. Tonight the real journey begins.

CHAPTER 19 - THEIR JOURNEY INTO THE REAL

Cassie knew the group looked to her as the leader in this time of discovery. Consequently, she was the one that called her friends together to work out the best plan for preparation; even if was only a formality born of her desire make sure everyone felt part of a consensus decision. Cassie had the plan for preparation they would follow carefully detailed in her mind. All she needed was co-operation. She had no doubt it would be hers.

Cassie walked purposefully into the kitchen to join her friends at the kitchen table. "Is there any coffee?" she asked and everyone cracked up as Cassie pulled out a chair and sat down. "What?" she asked as though innocent of the 'good cuppa Joe' incident. Cassie smiled widely and joined the laughter. Enjoying this light moment with Frankie and all of her friends she accepted the glass of orange juice from Max; he had quickly poured one for her and had set it in front of her. Somehow he knew Cassie would probably never drink a cup of coffee again; at least not by choice he chuckled to himself.

Picking up her glass of orange juice, Cassie looked around the table into the faces of Frankie, Key, Max, Ryan, and Kyle and smiled widely at the antics of each. Frankie was pulling the wool over Max's eyes with a plausible explanation, Key was giggling while he fed Cheerios to Willy, and Ryan and Kyle were alternately elbowing one another whenever a really good fart joke could be grossly told and thoroughly enjoyed. One by one they stopped horsing around and sat up attentively in their chairs and quietly turned toward Cassie. She sat at the table with a wistful smile formed on her lips and their place in tomorrow shining in her eyes. There was a compelling energy in the room and it seemed to be coming from Cassie.

Cassie mentally shook off her introspection and said, "You all know we have a *lot* to do before we can load'em up and head'em out, right? Cassie asked as she looked into the eyes of each. She realized that they were a family now and it would take all of her strength to put a stop to the possibility of losing any one of them. "A lot to do! Right! Lots lady! Too true!" they chorused unanimously. "Hey, hey," Cassie said in a laughing voice, "One at a time you guys or my brain is going to explode."

"Listen," said Cassie, "I have a plan and I'd like to tell you what I think we need to do to get ready. Is that OK?" asked Cassie.

"Sure," said Frankie reaching over to give Cassie's hand a loving squeeze before pulling back to listen. No one questioned Frankie's response and they waited attentively to hear what Cassie had to say.

"Right," said Cassie, "I'll start with the obvious and then the less obvious. You can stop me any time, but please hear me without interruption if possible, OK?" Cassie was pleased to see her newly perceived family members nodding in agreement. She outlined her plan.

"First we need to go to our rooms, strip off our clothing for laundering, and then take showers. Don't look so modest Ryan, there are robes for each of us in our rooms and we can wear them while our clothes are washed and dried. Oh! Go through your pockets and put your treasures in a pile and include belts, shoes, and anything else you've been carrying around. Put all of your washables outside of your bedroom door, please. Abigail has assured me they will be collected and laundered immediately afterward. When we have all showered and robed up, we'll meet back here for a delicious lunch Abigail has offered to prepare for us. "So far so good," thought Cassie. "After lunch we meet in the library after returning to our rooms to bring along everything we brought with us that did not go into the laundry piles. I have a feeling we will need some items we already have to complete our journey. *"Don't ask me how I know; I just do,"* thought Cassie. She looked into their rapt faces and asked, "What do you say we start with that as the first part of our preparation plan and I'll outline the second part when we get settled in the library after lunch. Will we follow my plan? Does everyone agree with my ideas?" Cassie asked anxiously, praying no one else would have another plan in mind to counter hers.

"I no have things, Lady," informed Key.

"That's fine Key," she smiled, "but it is important for us to be clean and comfortable when we start out, so *you* too will have a shower and laundered clothing. *"I have a feeling this preparation is an important part of our journey; in some part of me, I sense this is part of a purification ceremony we have to follow,"* mused Cassie and further deepened the furrow of her brow. "The Guardians are

2

waiting for us," or rather me thought Cassie. "Let's not be a group of vagabonds showing up at their door looking for a handout; let's arrive with clear minds, clean bodies, and faith in humanity." There were nods all around and the boys began to drift from the room to follow the first part of Cassie's plan. Cassie rose and walked to her room to prepare. Plans, actions, hopes, deeds, and potential failure rushed back and forth in her thoughts like a manic tornado. "Just let it all go," thought Cassie as she slowly closed the door into her bedroom.

Cassie walked into the library and saw Max, Frank, Ryan, and Kyle sitting self-consciously on the floor in their floor length white robes. Key was standing on one of the chairs facing the fireplace looking over the back to inspect its intricate carving. The boys shifted uncomfortably and it fell to Key to say, "Lady. Chair for you. All we clean." Key's eyes fell and he continued to look at the carvings there. Cassie completed her walk to the chair and then she sat down. In front of the fireplace between boys were the bits and pieces each had brought in shirt pockets and jeans pockets when they made their mad dash from the youth hostel the night Ms. Ford was murdered. Cassie had all that she had pocketed before they had to flee and she placed items on the small table between the armchairs.

"When do you start chanting?" Cassie asked innocently. She was referring to the white floor length robes worn by the boys. The boys looked around at one another and then again down at themselves before Cassie's reference made any sense and they fell out in laughter.

"With all of our hair we can be the band *Rebel Monks!*" Max enthused from his spot leaning against the wall directly next to the fire pit opening. Frankie sat on the floor next to Max and pulled on Max's robe ties; it annoyed Max and amused Frankie.

Seeing Max and Frankie starting an altercation it wasn't long before Ryan shouted, "Off with his head," indicating Kyle. Ryan stood leaning against the opposite side of the fire pit from Max and he reached onto the fireplace mantle and brandished a fire poker at the prone Kyle. Kyle jumped to his feet to find a weapon and the chase around the room was on and Key was off of the chair in a flash to join in the fun. Seeing the now empty armchair resulted in Max and Frankie landing side by side in a tangle of limbs in their efforts to be the first to claim the chair.

Cassie laughed helplessly as she looked at her family in its finest hour; choosing laughter over tears with so much negative possibility before them. "Hey, guys," Cassie spoke for attention. "There's an Xbox over here!" Cassie lied. Four heads snapped around to see where it could be. Key, of course, took this as his chance to win the game, whatever he thought it might be, by snatching the poker from Ryan and handing it to Kyle.

"It yours. Run fast, Key does. Try catching!" Key called over his shoulder as he streaked from the library and disappeared down the hallway.

Kyle shook his head and chuckled at the absurdity of their antics and assured everyone, "I won't be chasing him. He Key. He Fast!" Another round of laughter soon had everyone back to normal and Cassie knew it was time to take their plan to the next level.

"I have some good news from Constance," Cassie said. "Constance and Lucy are giving us each a backpack, flashlight, waterproof

KENNY FIGULY & LENNA FIGULY

matches, water, and preserved food for the journey. That backpack will be where you carry whatever won't fit into your pockets," Cassie explained. "Actually, the backpacks are over on the floor in front of that bookshelf." She motioned with her hand toward the proper bookshelf.

"Do you want me to bring them over?" offered Max.

"No thanks," said Cassie. "Let's each choose a pack, stow our gear, and place them near the library door to give us access."

Everyone agreed and it was while each packed their own pack that Key charged into the library, "Food time! Much pbjsamich! Treat, treat, treat, lady. Abigail promise. Abigail do. Come to eat. No polite wait," he chattered. Everyone laughed hearing Key's excited chatter.

"OK, Key," chuckled Cassie. "We'll be there in five minutes." Key charged back out of the library to let Ms. Lonely and Abigail of the horde about to arrive in the kitchen. "He went for the deviled eggs," thought Cassie. "I hope he saves me one."

The gear was finally packed and set near the library door when Kyle said, "How come Frankie's backpack looks like a turtle?"

Cassie laughed and said, "Where do you think Willie will ride when she isn't comfortable?" The light dawned in Kyle's eyes and he smiled at the visual of Willie riding shotgun over Frankie's shoulder from her nest in his backpack.

"Let's go," said Max, "I'm really hungry."

"OK Max," said Frankie, "I'll race you," he said while pushing Max away and running out of the library and down the hallway with Max, Ryan, Cassie, and Kyle in quick pursuit.

After a late lunch and cleanup, Cassie suggested they have a nap

174

until eleven that night. Yawning after a huge meal the boys agreed and everyone went to bed for a much needed sleep. When Cassie woke she found her laundered clothing folded at the foot of the bed and she got up and dressed. She knocked on doors until she knew the others were up and getting dressed. They all met in the library and put on their shoes and shouldered their packs, adjusting for maximum comfort. "This is it. We'll have a late supper and then start packing up to head out," stated Cassie. She led the way to the kitchen.

By the time the group was ready and packed for the journey it was nearly two in the morning. Everyone was rested, but they felt driven by anticipation and fear. As they entered a black Suburban SUV, loading the last of the supplies, the tension was great. This was real. They were heading for something of an adventure that could lead to life or death. It was the death part that concerned them the most.

Cassie was the last to enter the vehicle. She sat up front next to Constance. Constance seemed very sure of herself. She wanted to avoid any worry that her own doubts would cause. Everyone was ready. Constance drove the SUV out of the court yard and onto the only street that led back to Jerusalem.

"Would some music help the mood," offered Constance. Everyone looked around anticipating a single yes or no. Constance pressed a couple of buttons on the CD player. The song, *Anthem*, came blaring out of the speakers. Good Charlotte was one of Cassie's favorite bands. Constance was up to her old tricks again, of this Cassie was sure. How else would she know? The music lifted the mood enough to assist in conversation.

"This is an awesome song," said Kyle.

"Maybe we could listen to some AC/DC next," offered Max.

"Just as long as we stay away from anything depressing," said Cassie.

Willie, who was busy in the back trying to get comfortable, seemed to enjoy the music thoroughly. She rocked back and forth to the beat. Everyone found it quite comical. A dancing spider that dug punk rock music; does it get any more bizarre?

"Their earlier music was better," said Kyle.

"Whatever," stated Cassie, "Every artist reveals parts from their lives into the songs and lyrics on their CDs. You have to look deeper than just the music and the lyrics. You have to find the meaning behind each song. For me it's like getting to know the artist in a fractured, faceted sort of way."

"Good for you Cass, a rock critic at heart," said Frankie. Cassie could not help smiling. Her brother was always there to take her side. He would always have her heart.

"AC/DC," Max repeated.

"Can it, Max!" said Ryan. "I like this. Besides, the only reason you ever grew to love AC/DC was because you read once that Stephen King was a fan." Ryan laughed, breaking the tension even more so.

"Don't be naughty boys," said Constance with patient smile. "We have a long drive ahead of us, giving us time to listen to all of your favorites."

"So how many CD's are stacked in that player of yours?" Ryan asked.

"An endless number," said Constance. No one doubted her answer. They were not on a safe journey, but somehow they felt lucky to have an endless supply of good music as a cushion between the wondering about and then the knowing about when they arrived at their destination.

"Did you know that drinking coffee can give you butt cancer?" offered Kyle." No one understood the context of the information. It was funny, though.

"Colon cancer," corrected Constance.

"If you don't poop you'll die and if you do poop you die. It's inevitable," offered Max.

"That's very astute," rejoined Constance.

"Really? Butt jokes at a time like this. Will it ever end with you guys?" demanded Cassie.

"Come on Cassie, where's that wicked sense of humor hiding?" asked Frankie, grinning ear to ear.

"I'm busy being in the moment," she answered.

Max put his hand on Cassie's shoulder, reassuring her. More precisely he was reassuring himself in the process.

"Join the living for a moment," said Frankie.

"Poor choice of words Frank," replied Cassie.

"I guess I just miss that great smile of yours. We're in this together. Come hell or high water we're going to get through this."

"I'm sorry Frank. I just can't right now." Cassie leaned forward, studying the shadows in the dark. She wanted something more. She was sure of that. This was an odd fate all the way around. She couldn't decide if she was having second thoughts or simply stressed.

One thing was certain; Frank kept her from losing her mind. He was her rock in a sea of darkness. Then, of course, there was Max; one of her best friends. Strangely, she had recently felt an odd sense of closeness to him. Sure he was attractive in a mop-headed basketball jock sort of way, but even his little quirks were beginning to grow on her. The fact remained; he was Frankie's *best* friend. Creating rifts and breaks in that relationship was the only reason she could turn Max from her attention to avoid that situation.

"No need for apologies, Sis."

"I love you Frankie." Cassie reached around to pat her brother on the leg. He put his hand on hers. Max glanced down at Cassie's hand, wishing she had said the same words to him.

"Okay everybody, we're about to enter the city. Don't worry about having to show ID's at the check point."

Sure enough they passed the guards at the check point as if they were invisible to them. No one questioned the reasons. They were catching on quickly. Constance had a way about her that no one doubted. She meant business.

"She has awesome *Star Wars* Jedi moves," whispered a wide-eyed Kyle into Max's ear.

Max laughed. He'd been thinking the same thing. Constance was a powerful being to reckon with. She was the Mother of all things. Her power was endless and unquestionably indisputable.

"Your thoughts are quite amusing, Maxwell," said Constance from the driver's seat.

Max quickly quieted his mind. She was Luke Skywalker and Obi-Wan Kenobi all rolled into one.

After about twenty minutes they arrived in Old Jerusalem. The streets were cold and vacant. Cassie grew leery of every movement outside of the SUV. The shadows played tricks on her mind. She tried to remember she was safe for the time being. Within minutes the headlights struck the Well of Souls, casting a finality of the moment in everyone's hearts and minds.

Constance stopped the vehicle and took a deep breath, stretched and put her hands back on the steering wheel, gripping it tight. She wasn't one to worry but she'd grown close to these children, these young people with the potential for so much in front of them. She loved them all. Each one for different reasons: Cassie for her strength of character, Frankie for his loving support of his sister, Max for his humor even in the darkest of moments, Kyle and Ryan for their love of each other as friends, tiny Key for his innocence. These were the people who were chosen, and they had been chosen well.

"Listen please," started Constance with a hint of melancholy in her voice, "This will be the true beginning of your journey together. The way is dangerous and full of pitfalls. I have faith in each and every one of you." She took another deep breath, allowing the emotion to show. "Aside from Key and Willie, this will be the last time we will ever see one another. I adore you. And you, Cassie, will carry my spirit in your heart during the long arduous journey ahead and forever after. Key, take care of them… you and Willie. Your job is just as important as theirs. Key remained speechless. Willie crawled over the seats to sit in Constance's lap.

Cassie looked over at Constance, who was busy staring down at Willie with tears in her eyes.

"I wish I could take this journey with you. I truly do," said Constance quietly. "You are the sons and daughter of the old kings. This may not make much sense to you now. You will grow to understand what this means. I'm not hiding the truth from you I just don't have the words. You must all discover for yourselves the meaning in life that you carry. It wouldn't be fair. I don't want to be your regrets. This is all that you have. But I will give what I have to you in prayer for your safety. Trust me; you will have what you need. I have already made sure of that."

"I feel reckless and clumsy," said Cassie. "Am I coming back from...?" She stopped herself from completing the words.

"You have already made your way back, Cassie," said Constance with a smile. "This is just another beginning."

"It's making my heart spin, Constance," Cassie confided. She closed her eyes and opened the door, stepping out into the cool night air. Opening her eyes to a very dim light she shut the door and walked to the back of the vehicle pulling the doors open wide. Her pack was the last to go in so it was on top of the rest. "I can be constant and faithful in my devotion," she whispered to herself as she lifted the small pack and slung it around her shoulders. This journey would be fueled by devotion and each would carry their portion at all times for use in case of peril. "Pray God," Cassie thought, "No peril would be encountered by anyone but her.

Willie and the boys jumped out soon after. They were busy making their goodbyes. Upon these voyages of unearthing a strange reality, as they would someday call them, they were to them real voyages through an amazing space in history. It was almost prophecy, that the secrets they held were held in private places within their individual minds.

"It's hard to heed the warning when you cannot see the crime," said Cassie to no one in particular.

"What's that, Sis?" asked Frankie.

"Nothing important."

"Do you ever feel like a stranger here?" she asked him. Frankie wasn't sure what she meant. The question seemed out of character. Of course they were strangers here. They were in another country. However, something told him the question was deeper than that.

"We are strangers here in so many ways," he replied.

"Strangers or not, our being here will have a positive effect or the loss of humanity is going to go beyond that of God's wrath after Noah set sail. *I* don't see our importance here, but there are voices in my head, Frankie. They sound so far away they could be from another Universe and I am constantly hearing that background of voices telling me that I *am*, that *we* are, of enormous importance; the only option left to save humanity. Frankie, I've been chosen for a task I believe I can achieve with help from everyone. I have no reason to believe I'm anything special, but when Mother Earth and Lucifer give you your marching orders then it lends a little more weight to the believability side of the scale; but I still feel so alone."

"In some ways you're right, Cass. In some ways each of us is here alone. That's what dad used to say when he was deep in thought."

"What do you suppose he meant by that," she asked.

"I think he was talking about individualism. About how we all have our own loads to bear, you know? I don't think we should or can expect to find miracles to save us; we have to save ourselves," said Frankie.

Cassie knew that Frankie was referring to the road ahead. His words felt dark to her, as if they might fail the mission. But failing was out the question. She'd already played it over in her mind many times. The argument, the terror along the way, the possible loss, and these things were not scary to her any longer. They were the reality. She wasn't looking for miracles.

What if life was the miracle?

What if they were here only to borrow this living energy for a short time?

Cassie cleared her mind. She put her back pack down for a moment and unzipped the side pocket, pulling from it a flash light. The beam of light lit up the short trial leading to the Well of Souls. So far so good, there was no sign of those wretched shadow men. Once everyone had vacated the vehicle they followed suit, pulling out their flashlights.

Cassie thumbed through the first of the nine journals, studying the hand drawn picture her father had made of the area. She examined the picture and then shone the beam of light to the side of the well of souls. It was there plain as day; a single rock that was clearly out of place along the top of the entrance. It was the key-hole. She didn't want to say anything at first, her excitement brimming over with enthusiasm.

They waited until Constance drove away leaving them standing alone in the dark. Events were final. It was time to move ahead with nothing but nine journals and their wits about them. Cassie was feeling quite brave. She walked straight to the odd shaped rock, took a deep breath and, without further explanation, she pulled it free from the wall.

"Key, I need your small hands," said Cassie.

Key jumped to attention. He knew, without being told, what to do. He reached inside the empty hole where the rock once was placed and gave a push. The entire wall vibrated as a single small crawl space opened.

"This is it," stated Cassie. "All we have to do is move forward." No one hesitated. They had come this far and intended to go farther. Key led the way as they entered the crawl space. Frankie was followed quickly by a skittering Willie. Ryan and Kyle followed expressionlessly behind. Only Max and Cassie had yet to enter the crawl space. "After you my lady," Max said pretending to doff his feathered hat and extend it to her on one bent knee. Cassie laughed a huge belly laugh that seemed to lighten her fears and buoy her spirits. "Sir Max. I will accept your offer and gladly," Cassie thanked him. As soon as she and Max entered the small cavern through the crawl space the door slid shut. Cassie decided to leave the journals in the cavern; they could serve no further use. They were no longer physically needed. Whatever the journals had revealed about making the journey to the Guardians would be carried in Frankie's, Max's, and her minds. God help them if anyone forgot an important lesson; in school they would get bad marks... in here they would get bad dead.

CHAPTER 20 - THE LONG WALK
THROUGH PERDITION

Cassie led them all from the small cavern into a spacious cavern whose roof was lost in darkness and where all that their flashlights could illuminate was a large pool of water at the far end of the cavern and to the left of the cavern, a ledge path leading up from the cavern floor.

Ryan and Kyle began to run down to the pool of water slashing flashlight beams through the air toward each other in an attempt to produce light saber effects as they pretended to be Galactic troopers in search of Luke Skywalker. Cassie watched them play and an uneasy feeling began to grow in the pit of her stomach. She was forgetting something very important right this minute.

"Let me be a Jedi Knight for a while," shouted Kyle from the edge of the pool and just as he and Ryan crossed light-swords an enormous backwash of water came from the pool and Cassie's blood ran cold with recollection; the Teneculum! That was what she had forgotten. Her father's journal had included a warning to stay on the ledge path side of the cavern and to begin the journey up the ledge and to avoid the pool where the giant octopod waited to feed.

"Come back!!!" she shouted and waved as she ran swiftly toward the pool. "Kyle! Ryan! Get away from the water! Run to me as fast as you can," Cassie screamed for their attention as she sprinted toward their location and then it was upon them.

While the remainder of the group stood at the base of the ledge path talking about the best order to proceed up the ledge, Cassie's screams echoed and re-echoed through the cavern. Max and Frankie ran swiftly to Cassie and the three of them saw an enormous sinuous tentacle reach out of the pool and ensnare Ryan's leg; swinging him high above the pool into the darkness above.

"Get back, Kyle," shouted Max and Frankie in unified frustration as they sprinted down toward the pool. There was another dark tentacle slithering along the ground toward Kyle's leg and he missed seeing it in his panic to do something to save Ryan. Willie was riding partially up on Frank's shoulder to see what was happening, Max pounded alongside Frank. Key stood statue still when he saw the beast begin to rise in the middle of the pool below the ensnaring tentacle. Key knew exactly what to do.

Key cupped his hands around his mouth and shouted, "Willie! Call brothers and sisters!"

Cassie stood horrified as she watched Ryan being waved back and forth struggling to pry the encircling tentacle from his body. Cassie dreaded what would happen if the sinuous arm dragged Ryan underwater. Max and Frankie had reached Kyle just as the seeking tentacle touched his ankle and they kept running while scooping Kyle up with one boy on each side carrying him away. "Cassie?" shouted

Frankie while running away from the water with Kyle safely flying between his and Max's arms as they ran, "Where is it safe?"

"Go to the ledge!" shouted Cassie just as Key streaked past her toward the far wall where Willie waited. "Come back, Key!" Cassie shouted to the tiny boy pumping his arms and legs as fast as they would carry him.

"Help me! Help me, Kyle! Anyone! It's starting to squeeze meeeeeeeeeeee," screamed Ryan as he was waved lower in the air than before on what looked like a sure dunking into the pool by the Teneculum.

"Where's Willie?" Frank shouted to Cassie anxiously as he and Max reached the ledge and held fast to Kyle who struggled furiously to get back to Ryan.

"She and Key are over by the far cavern wall, Frankie! It looks like they're working on something!" shouted Cassie. "What are we going to do for Ryan?" she cried out in frustration.

Key streaked back from the far wall to Cassie who stood halfway between the ledge path and the far wall. Key told Cassie, "Willie call brothers and sisters. We go to water. We dance, we yell, we get eye on us; Willie know what. Willie smart she is. We go to her."

"Help me Kyle!" screamed Ryan as the Teneculum waved him closer to itself and the water. "Please, God! Someone help me!"

Cassie motioned to Max, Frankie, and Ryan to follow her and they raced behind her and caught up to her near the pool. "What do we do, Cassie, what do we do?" Kyle screamed at her. "That, that..."

"It's called a Teneculum... remember Frankie, from dad's journals? Anyway, Key told me that we need to get its attention by jumping up

and down and taunting it in any way to keep it from dunking Ryan."
Kyle immediately ran up to the shoreline looking for things to throw
while screaming and jumping up and down.

"Where *is* Key and where's Willie? She jumped out when Max and
I grabbed Kyle, said Frank.

"Key and Willie have something cooking guys, so let's be noisy bait
while we wait for whatever they have in mind," suggested Cassie as
she began to run down to the pool shore followed and then passed
by Frankie and Max.

"We're working on getting you safe, Ryan!" shouted Frankie as
he shot a rock at the Teneculum's bulbous middle for fear of hitting
Ryan.

Cassie, Frankie, Max, and Kyle whirled like dervishes, threw
missiles like Zulu warriors, hollered and shrieked, and kept it up while
shouting encouragement to Ryan who was looking terrified and pain
filled.

Key and Willie did what was second nature. Key kept his new
family busy and reasonably safe from the blind and deaf Teneculum
in the pool. Willie consulted with Mother Earth in clicks and cheeps
in a language that was ancient before humanity first arrived on the
scene. Soon a virtual army of giant hairy spiders of the Gaia Clan
began to cover the walls; clicking, cheeping, and making plans to
save Ryan. Suddenly, the caverns only sounds came from Key's family
down near and in the pool. Instantly every member of the Gaia Clan
began to move in on the Teneculum.

Key ran down toward the pool to pull his family aside while Willie
went in with the Cavalry.

"Don't leave me here you guys!" screamed Ryan and then he saw Willie. She skittered over the surface of the water without breaking its tension, ran up the bulbous side of the Teneculum, clittered up the tentacle holding Ryan and then ran up his body wrapping eight articulated arms around his back and shoulders. Ryan had never been so relieved. True, he was still wrapped in a tentacle waving through the air like a demented whirl-a-gig at the carnival, but if Willie was here it meant that he had help and his heart began to slow from its paradiddle rhythm.

In the hours ahead they would speak in wonderment of the thousands of Willie's Clan eight-legging it all *over* the Teneculum releasing their toxin into it and causing it to unfurl Ryan and Willie onto the shore. They would ask again and again to see the imprints of the Teneculum on Ryan's body. That day would become legendary in their years ahead, but in that moment they would, each in his, or her, own way, thank Mother Earth for keeping her promise of hope and help throughout their journey.

The journey along the ledge leading to the Council room of the Guardians was Cassie's responsibility and she led her family single-file along the way she was illuminating with her flashlight. Key was happily running ahead to scout the way with Willie clittering after him and riding his shoulder when he returned to the main group. Max strode warily behind Cassie, poking his light into every nook and cranny of the spaces being passed. Ryan and Kyle were sandwiched between Max and Frankie so they could keep an eye on Ryan; he had suffered greatly mere hours before.

They had been steadily climbing the ledge path for several

hours, stopping to drink water and munch on some preserved food occasionally whenever Frankie called for a rest stop. Cassie had asked Frankie to keep an eye on the boys. Their confrontation with the Teneculum had taken a heavy toll on Ryan's strength and Kyle's self-confidence; Kyle would not leave Ryan's side. Frankie called for a rest break and Ryan immediately slid boneless down the wall; it was as if Ryan were a marionette whose strings had suddenly been cut. Kyle immediately sat down beside him. As Frank carefully walked the ledge around the boys and Max up to Cassie at the front of the line he noticed Ryan's pallor and glazed eyes and reported them to Cassie and Max as they settled down for a rest. Cassie knew that time was of the essence, but she was certain that live or die they were all supposed to make the journey and that the Guardians knew they were on the way. World time was meaningless to *them*. Cassie would make it to her destination or not as the Universe willed during whatever time-space was available.

"I don't want to seem callous about this Frankie, but part of the deal is that we have *all* have been chosen for this; Constance herself could not see our way. This may be some cosmic joke, but any or all of us could fall on this trail; hurt and dying. The rest of us must go on. No matter how few of us remain we have to keep making the attempt to reach the Council room of the Guardians until we are successful or lying dying on this ledge; not unknown, or forgotten, but lost in death to those outside of these walls," summarized Cassie.

Frankie and Max had laid their flashlights down to illuminate the ledge and the supplies in the packs where their water and preserved food awaited them. The shadows from the light seemed to walk through Cassie's eyes as they gave her their full attention while wrapping their minds around what Cassie had just said. Frank and Max had known there would be in danger, but what passed for danger in here was exponentially more horrifying than they could have imagined; dead and dying lying littered in their wake had not been remotely believable when they had been told it could happen. Cassie dropped her eyes to her pack and she began to methodically get her water and preserved food out of it. Her flashlight kept getting in her way as she reached into her pack so she put the 'light loop around her wrist and continued to prepare a snack before it was time to continue.

Key tore around the bend ahead screaming, "Willie called Clan. Danger, danger, danger! The Guardian Clan comes!" just as Gaia Clan members dropped onto the backs of Cassie and the members of her family. An eerie susurration rose in volume from the bend ahead and suddenly the Guardian Clan giant hairy spiders fell on them. In the ensuing struggle packs and flashlights disappeared into the depths beside the ledge. Cassie stood wildly weaving to give her Gaia Clan protector his best chance to dispatch the giant hairy spider attacking her. The wildly swinging flashlight on the end of her arm was the only light in the cavern and in the shadows of battle it would illuminate first one then another of the struggles going on around her. "Help us, Gaia!" Cassie shouted out in her mind, but the wildly waving flash played out only strobe-like flashes of deadly fights for life going on up and down the ledge. The battle was waged for what seemed to be an eternity of time and then it was suddenly, violently, over.

"Where is everyone," shouted Cassie shining her light down the ledge. "Is everyone OK? Shout out guys!" cried Cassie while her stomach twisted in a knot of worry and potentially devastating grief. Cassie ran up to the top of the ledge path and turned the corner and she could see faint light at the apex of the ledge beaconing her and her family to their destination. Faintly, from behind her Cassie could hear voices responding to her pleas and she raced back down the ledge to gather whoever remained and lead them around the corner of the ledge and up to their destination. It was many hours later before the brave little band of travelers started around the turn in the ledge path where they could see their destination for themselves.

Leading all of her family up the last portion of the ledge, the door to the Council room of 'The Guardians of the Garden' came into view and Cassie led the way for the last of her family's journey. As they slowly walked, limped, and struggled up to the Council room door the light of billions of phosphorus creatures lit the way toward their destination like an upside-down night sky sprinkled liberally with emerald green stars. Looking back toward the way they had come, Cassie noticed the return path was no longer a pit of dank darkness; just dim emerald green light along the path.

As they reached the Council room door a commanding voice boomed, "Send in humanities representative. The rest of you are to leave the way you came and await events as they transpire." Essentially, Cassie had been called to action and her family had been invited to leave. Cassie let out a deep breath. She did not realize she had not been breathing for fear of what would become of her companions. Cassie's heart sang with the knowledge that danger, deprivation, and fear would be absent during her family's return to Jerusalem.

CHAPTER 21 - DEFENDING HUMANITY

Just outside of the burnished gold doorway into the Council room of 'The Nine Guardians of the Garden', Cassie stood silently with her family. She knew she would enter alone and that everyone else would go back through the Well of Souls to the Tomb of the Virgin to wait for her return. She knew they would wait for her as long as was necessary. At this point in their journey no one doubted that Cassie would succeed in her defense of humanity; not even Cassie.

Cassie motioned to Frankie to step aside with her for a private moment. Her eyes filled with tears as she looked lovingly at her brother. His clothes were dirty and torn, he wore his belt as a sling to support his painful left arm, and where his skin wasn't dirty it was scraped and raw. "You will know I'm fine Frankie," said Cassie softly in reference to their special link of twin communication. Frankie's eyes were shining with unshed tears and Cassie pretended not to notice.

"It's time for you to go in Cass," Frankie said as he moved forward and gave his sister a one-armed hug that seemed to last forever and no time at all. His tears overflowed and left vertical streaks on his grubby face, but he did not cry. "I think it's time to, say good-bye for now, Sis," Frankie said as he stepped back from their hug. He held her hand as they took the few steps back to the others.

"I need to get going guys," said Cassie as she stood holding Frankie's hand. She looked at each of her family and noted Key's black eye and torn clothing, Willie's broken pincher, Max's shredded shirt and the underlying deep scratches on his arms and neck, Ryan's bruised and battered face and body, and Kyle's matching condition. Cassie could feel the tiny fractures in her heart that had occurred with each wounding of her family as they had fought bravely to see her to this place.

"Take care, Sis," said Frankie as they dropped hands and hugged once more. "Try," he said smiling in an attempt to lift the mood, "Not to take too long saving the world."

Cassie walked over to Key standing quietly with Willie riding in the backpack that had been Frankie's at the beginning of their journey. She crouched down in front of Key and Willie and said, "Thank you both for saving our lives." She lifted her hand and scratched the part of Willie's tummy she could reach and then caressed her broken pincher and received a loving nip in return. Key looked into her eyes and as Cassie reached over to ruffle his hair, he moved into her arms and hugged her tightly around the waist.

"Lady brave. Smarter and smarter. Have perfect pbjsamich trip. No worry. We see soon, lady," Key said releasing her from what had become a shared hug. "I take care all. For you, lady. All safe back." Cassie knew they would have no trouble going back and she took Key up on his offer to take care of the boys on the return journey.

Ryan and Kyle were leaning shoulder to shoulder in pain and exhaustion when Cassie walked up and gave both boys a gentle group hug and her thanks for their courage and steadfastness. "I'll need to hear some good fart jokes when I get back, so you guys get some rest when you get out of here and wrack your brains for the best ones you know because I'll be looking forward to hearing them," she said when she removed her arms from their shoulders.

"Be careful Cassie," they spoke softly in unison. Under the circumstances their usual rejoinder of, "You owe me a coke!" said in unison was absent but everyone else gently laughed at the number of cokes each imagined Ryan and Kyle probably owed to one another; in unison was their normal mode of conversation.

Finally, Cassie approached Max. "You look like you walked through a shredder, Maxie," she said as they shared a sad smile. Cassie wanted to reach up and touch the deep scores on his neck where the mandibles of one of the Guardian Clan giant hairy spiders had scored him. His Gaia Clan protector had fallen in battle and Max had single handedly fought the venomous Guardian Clan giant spider into submission. Willie had disposed of it efficiently and without a single sound. "Will you take care of Frankie for me?" Cassie asked.

Max shyly reached out and pulled Cassie toward him and gave her what he hoped seemed like a brotherly hug. Max whispered in Cassie's ear, "I will Cass. I'll take care of Frankie." Cassie and Max slowly moved away from one another and Max's worry for Cassie shone in his eyes.

"Please don't worry about me, Max. I'll just do what I came to do and then meet you back at the Tomb of the Virgin, or wherever." Max nodded and walked over to adjust Frankie's belt-sling.

"I have to go now," said Cassie and without a backward glance she pushed at the Council room door and it swung open to admit her. Outside the boys were already moving steadily away.

The Council room of The Nine shone with golden light. Cassie stood at the edge of the room near the entrance behind a substantial marble table. She couldn't help but feel overwhelmed emotionally. Something larger than imaginable was rising from the depths of her sub-conscience; rising like a sea leviathan through the translucent surface to breathe.

From the corner of the marble table she could see a Persian rug where a large statue stood so beautiful and flame-like that it cast fantastic shadows across the long silk curtains that were stretched in front of a vast hallway. A subtle hint of voices passed through the whispering silk; like echoes in a dream. The dull roar of a Niagara of thoughts clouded her reason causing her to wonder if her words would become the miracle mankind needed to be saved, or the reason behind their extinction on Earth.

One of Nine spoke first. His voice was full and much louder than expected. The reverberation in the room caused Cassie's heart to skip a beat. He stood. The immense presence of his life force was undeniable.

"Speak, young woman," said One of Nine. Two and Three of Nine sat forward in their thrones, anticipating Cassie's words. Their faces appeared to be made of alabaster – snowy white marble. Their lips were stony, honey colored and lacking passion.

"My father wrote about you. He said you had the answers for all of humanity." Cassie said in wonderment and fear.

"Yes, he did," One of Nine spoke gravely. "He was confused and obsessive."

"You didn't know him," retorted Cassie. Her voice sounded small and useless inside the colossal great-room.

"We are aware of all things," said One of Nine. "Impatience doesn't lend well to your argument."

"Spare us your lack of restraint and total disregard for protocol," said Three of Nine. "What exactly do you wish to say?"

"I've come to you to beg forgiveness. I've come to beg you to allow humanity one more chance," Cassie replied steadily.

"Consider," requested Cassie, "Humanity is the architect of imaginative beauty. It's dismissive for you to interpret some of humanities tendencies toward violent nature to be the one and only face of mankind. Many turn to violence foolishly, like a small child who doesn't understand the fire and burns her hands trying to play with flames. Would you take her life simply because of her ignorance? Consider our conscious effort to recognize the ideal; to strive to create and appreciate beautiful things. There is the hope that mankind does offer. His awareness does exist. You can't look under the rock of humanity and see only the creatures fearing the light and decide only the place under the rock is where all of humanity writhes; look for the ugly, but for the sake of balance you must also look for the beautiful. It's true; evil lurks in the hearts of man. I'll be the first to admit it." Cassie took a deep breath, fighting to hold back her tears.

"You cannot expect to sway us through an emotional tirade of what might happen," countered three of nine. "We are here to protect this planet, not you and your brethren."

"Be careful or you'll dismiss your own argument by hiding behind excuses," said One of Nine. "You seem to be projecting a landslide of human kindness as your own reflection of what could be," he continued. "This court will not recognize memory, hope, or idealization as arguments. Your species is under scrutiny. The actions of mankind are ever more morbid and yet each of you has it within you to sprout flowers in the Garden instead of thorns; all of the information mankind needs to work out human issues in a non-violent ways has always been readily available. Mankind has been blessed with many gifts. Thought and language are gifts of communication; are instruments of an art you seem incapable of mastering. Humanities vices provide lyrics and humanities virtues provide melody for the song of your language. That song has become quite ugly. It concerns us that your gift of thought has not been cultivated. By this time in the Garden, humanity should have progressed to a point where it is capable of just not showing up when someone declares war; yes even to a point where war is no longer an option. "

Seven of Nine; his gowns blazing a bright incandescent green spoke reassuringly, "You, Cassie, are not on trial. However, be warned. Your words matter as much as your position here before this court. We are not your judge and jury as contradictory as this appears to be. We are a jury of Guardians judging the results of humanities use and care of the Garden. Show us with your words what is new, complex, and vital about mankind. We are concerned," he explained and every one of the other nine nodded their heads. "Understand Cassie, when people and groups of people disagree they have the option of working through the disagreement or of destroying one another. We can mourn the results of the symptom but not the cause of the disease."

Seven of Nine's words tore at her heart. They went far deeper than she was prepared to feel. In her head she wasn't arguing the truth she was arguing the reality of change; the magnitude of change necessary for the kind of growth of humanity required to convince the Guardians to allow for mankind's continued existence upon the Earth. It was because of this that a slow parade of thoughts and argumentative approaches occurred to her yet left her afraid and in awe of the adversaries standing before her.

Was she intelligent enough to face their counter arguments?

What about the world? Would it survive if she failed?

What had Lucifer said regarding fear? Fear would destroy her if she let it sink in!

Cassie felt like a tightrope walker in an endless carnival. She felt blinded being in the spotlight of truth; alternately thrilled and terrified by the idea that she was the only one there to stand witness for the continuance of humanity.

One of Nine smiled, bent over, plucked a strand of yellow silk from his robe and examined it. "I am quite sure I shall understand your position. We are not unreasonable," he replied, intently studying the little golden thread. "As for believing things, I can believe anything, provided that it is credible." He smiled again, only this time his smile allowed some warmth to escape his otherwise cool demeanor.

"My argument isn't just about humanity; it's about understanding

Humanity and the reasons behind the actions we have taken, are taking, and plan to take. There's beauty in kindness and it looks kind of ugly in here to me. Respectfully, I need to know; do you want us to fail to meet your standards?" said Cassie. "Don't you see the other side of this disagreement we have about the existence of mankind? The good that man has done has to mean something! There are those so dedicated to peace they gave their lives."

"You are asking to put your hands into the fire," said Six of Nine.

"Are you afraid of burning if you fail?" commented One of Five.

"Are you asking me if I'm willing to die for this cause? If so, the answer is yes," said Cassie backing up a few inches to allow her answer to carry more weight. She wondered to herself if it was true. Was death so bad a fate? It was, after all, inevitable.

A curious sensation of terror came over her. She knew that she had come face to face with beings whose mere nature was so absorbing that, if allowed to do so, it would absorb her entire soul.

"If you did not want any external influence in your life, why are you here? You know yourself, Cassie, how independent you are by nature. You have always been your own master," said One of Nine.

"I don't know how to explain it to you, said Cassie. " Something seemed to tell me that I was on the verge of a terrible crisis in my life. It wasn't about my father, although his loss affected the way I viewed my future.

"For one so delicate you have strongly borne your burdens," offered Seven of Nine.

"Thank you," said Cassie. "I want you to understand where I'm coming from; what I as a human understand. I didn't plan on making it this far. We fought hard to get here. I'm not even sure if I'll leave here alive. That realization clouds my ability to say what needs to be said." Cassie sighed and blinked, allowing her welling tears to finally fall. "I suppose," reflected Cassie, "It comes from the fact that none of us can stand each other's beliefs. As if having a differing opinion, belief or way of life will take something away from someone else. People having the same faults as one another can't quite sympathize with the indignation of dissimilarities. Human beings feel that evil should be their distinctive property. It's as if they have to empty out their own beliefs into a pool of billions. We, as a species, haven't learned to share. I don't believe it's a lack of love, or even goodness, it's a lack of tolerance." Cassie cleared her throat and wiped her tears on her sleeve. "Are you making your judgment based on your experience or on ours?" demanded Cassie.

"In the harsh struggle for existence you want to have something that measures your own personal gain," said One of Four. "That is your downfall. It's not about you. Your argument must include an ideal that serves all things great and small. You fill your minds with such disdain. Doesn't this concern you? After all, you are not the only one represented here! Greed has had her vicious teeth wrapped securely around your hearts for so long I fear you have lost the ability to understand your own history. You have been chosen to be eaten by the beast of gluttony and indifference while failing to consider an alternative based upon past experience; ignorance of your own history."

"Again," said Cassie, "Are we to be judged based upon humanities experience or that of a group of immortal beings with the ability to wipe mankind from the face of the Earth?" Cassie stood tall and willed herself to become as granite faced as mankind's jury.

"Cassie," began One of Eight, "the irony of this situation is that good and evil cannot exist without the other. That is simply a reality. You must have a basis for comparison. "

"That's my point exactly," blurted Cassie, "Balance. I want you to understand that even in the midst of war and famine selfless good can and does exist and provides that balance."

"Please share an example," Said One of Nine.

"It was you that admitted there must be balance, a basis for comparison. Well, that is the process through which we as humans learn to grow," said Cassie.

"That's far too easy," said One of Four.

One of Three snorted in agreement.

"A dangerous theory!" offered One of Two.

"What of free will?" Cassie asked.

"A dangerous precedent," said One of Two.

"Would you have it any other way?" One of Four asked with a twinge of cynicism.

"Why should it be any other way?" Cassie countered.

"Free will is a gift from your creator," offered One of Nine. "Humanity has used free will as an excuse to further every deadly agenda; eliminating compassion and grace.

"What is it you fear, Cassie? Death? The death of everyone? It is not something you should fear Cassie, rather it is something to embrace. Perhaps you are missing the greater theme? Free will is what allowed deceit amongst the thieves of perdition. If you allow your emotions to rule your life using free will to further your agenda the only outcome is anguish."

"Maybe the only reason that people like Adolf Hitler, Mussolini or Genghis Kahn existed was not the evil they caused to be committed but the compassion that grew from their bad example." Cassie took a deep breath. "Their bad examples and the horrors they perpetrated have allowed humanity to begin putting an end to the haters that have plagued mankind. Humankind lives in a state of grace that rises exponentially to armor us against the hatred we battle; the hatred we traded for life." Cassie did not know that her unwavering faith in the good of humanity was causing the Guardian's judgment of humanity to be noticed in the eternity of a higher power. Suddenly, Cassie could feel an electric-like boost clear her mind and make room for her final argument for the continuation of humanity; excitedly she visualized exactly how she must proceed.

"And what if you miscarry your own reasoning? What if humanity fails to propagate along the road you speak of?" said One of Nine.

Cassie was quick to answer. "What if you and the other eight were to simply vanish from the face of the Earth? What then? Would we be allowed to carry out our own burden of war and peace? Did you know Jesus, Mahatma Gandhi, Mother Teresa, or The Dali Lama? Did you make note of The Buddha and the Buddhist monks that live for the sake of peace alone. I'm not talking about worship; I'm talking about a force of benevolence so strong it has lasted since the beginning of man's search for meaning."

All nine guardians were speechless. The argument had finally come to a head. A decision must be made. The hidden source of dim golden light went black. Cassie held tightly to the edge of the granite table in order to keep herself balanced. The black was thick, leaving her breathless. The smell of Patchouli and Opium filled the air. Cassie could feel herself beginning to fade. She wasn't afraid to die. She had done what she knew had to be done. Then, in one final gasp for air, she fell to the ground and passed out.

When Cassie woke she was cold, choking down the cool air. She was lying at the foot of the Tomb of the Virgin. The sky was lit by a full moon and comforting stars filled the empty spaces. Then she saw them, her family. They looked stricken and joyful all at the same time.

"Where have you been? What was the argument?" were the first questions Cassie heard. Max was beside himself with worry as he helped Cassie carefully to her feet. Frankie, Kyle and Ryan rushed to her side as well. Key stood grinning with Willie peeping over Key's shoulder to see Cassie. "What you learn, lady?" asked Key through a shining smile.

"That love conquers all things great and small," Cassie whispered.

Turning to Max, Cassie smilingly held out her hands for him to take. "Max," Cassie said with tears streaming down her cheeks, "I learned about love." Max's eyes shone as he took her hands in his. Cassie leaned in and passionately kissed Max on his loving lips.

Behind the group an older man struggled up from the ground and started brushing dirt from his clothes and rubbing his glasses on his shirttail to clean them. As he placed his glasses on his face and studied the excitedly talking group in front of him he cleared his throat. "Excuse me," he said, as seven heads snapped around to look at him, "Do you know when it is?" he asked while rubbing the top of his head to further muss his hair. "Dad!!? Mr. Lint!!? Lady father?" Seven bodies hurtled toward the author of their journey.

THE END

Would you like to see your manuscript become a book?

If you are interested in becoming a PublishAmerica author, please submit your manuscript for possible publication to us at:

acquisitions@publishamerica.com

You may also mail in your manuscript to:

**PublishAmerica
PO Box 151
Frederick, MD 21705**

www.publishamerica.com